DOWNWARD
TOWARD DEMONS

Thus it was perverse impulse—anger at his uncle, and an even greater anger at the Gatekeepers—that sent Greylock downward; to seek not the cold bosom of the gods as was expected of him, but instead, to dare the warm clammy fingers of demons. Never before had any of his kind chosen to go down from Godshome. If ever his brethren left the safety of the High Plateau, it was always upward to the sacred snows of Godshome they made their pilgrimage; never into the dreaded and unknown depths of the Underworld. . . .

Also by Duncan McGeary

Star Axe

We will send you a free catalog on request. Any titles not in your local book store can be purchased by mail. Send the price of the book plus 50¢ shipping charge to Tower Books, P.O. Box 270, Norwalk, Connecticut 06825

Titles currently in print are available for industrial and sales promotion at reduced rates. Address inquiries to Tower Publications, Inc., Two Park Avenue, New York, New York 10016, Attention: Premium Sales Department.

SNOWCASTLES

Duncan McGeary

Fowler's Books
Buy - Sell - Trade
323 N. Euclid
Fullerton 92632
or
2634 W. Orangethorpe
Fullerton, 92634

TOWER BOOKS **NEW YORK CITY**

Maps for Snowcastles by Derry Timleck, B.F.A., M.Sc.A.E., M.A.A.E., Faculty of Education, University of Ottawa, Ottawa, Canada.

A TOWER BOOK

Published by

Tower Publications, Inc.
Two Park Avenue
New York, N.Y. 10016

THE LANDS OF GREYLOCK'S ADVENTURES

JOURNEY OF GREYLOCK ••••>••>••••

DERRY G. TIMLECK, JULY-1980

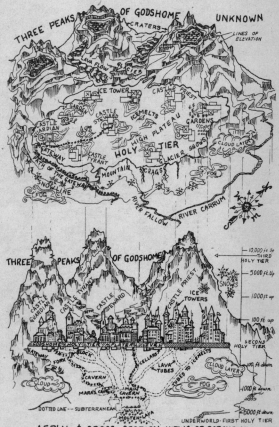

AERIAL & CROSS SECTION VIEWS OF GODSHOME

JOURNEY OF GREYLOCK••••••••

DERRY G. TIMLECK, JULY, 1980

REGION OF TWILIGHT DELLS
LAND OF WYRRS
JOURNEY OF GREYLOCK ••••

DERRY G. TIMLECK, JULY, 1980

REGION OF THE BORDERKEEP

JOURNEY OF GREYLOCK ······

DERRY G. TIMLECK, JULY, 1980

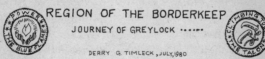

Chapter One

When Greylock descended the peaks of God-shome he was excited, yet strangely unafraid. The winds were cold and gusty, but he no longer cared—the harsh, pitiless message in his uncle's parting words colored his cheeks far more than the mountain winds ever could. At any other time he would have turned back, but now the words of the Tyrant still burned in his memory, and an angry, almost overwhelming resolve to prove his uncle wrong had cast out his last remaining fears of leaving the High Plateau. Exiled by his uncle, Greylock prepared to die. At times he looked over his shoulder, expecting with every glance to see the Tyrant's soldiers rushing down the steep slopes of

Godshome after him. Already his knife had tasted blood for the first time, and he wiped his hands desperately to remove the sticky, drying fluid; but it clung to the cracks of his hand.

Above Greylock loomed the mighty crags of the mountain, wherein dwelt the gods themselves. Below him were the hot humid valleys, unnaturally green and warm; where, it was said, demons lived. A familiar litany came to mind almost unbidden. "Only on the High Plateau is it good and right and proper for man to live"—so taught the Gatekeepers, priests of the High Plateau.

Thus it was perverse impulse—anger at his uncle, and an even greater anger at the Gatekeepers—that sent Greylock downward; to seek not the cold bosom of the gods as was expected of him, but instead, to dare the warm clammy fingers of demons. Never before had any of his kind chosen to go down from Godshome. If ever his brethren left the safety of the High Plateau, it was always upward to the sacred snows of Godshome they made their pilgrimage; never into the dreaded and unknown depths of the Underworld.

Like every child Greylock had learned the Holy Hierarchy of Tiers early in his life; drilled into him day after day by the gatekeepers. The Third Holy Tier, the lofty heights of Godshome, was the domain of the gods. The High Plateau was the Second Holy Tier of Existence, and the home of man. The First Tier of the Underworld, the Gatekeepers had taught, was the realm of demons. Greylock smiled grimly to himself. He was going where Keyholder had always said he would go, if a bit sooner than his old teacher had imagined!

Demons there may be, he thought, but it was his uncle's Steward he feared the most at this moment. When Carrell Redfrock discovered the direction his prey had escaped, there would undoubtedly be pursuit. Next in the line of succession by virtue of his office, the Steward would not rest until he was certain that the only surviving blood heir was truly dead. Greylock knew that the Steward no more believed in demons or gods than he did, but Carrell Redfrock would be relying on the cold ice of God-shome to rid him of his rival. He would not be certain of the deadliness of the Underworld's mythical denizens.

His uncle, the Tyrant, had long ago fallen under the sway of the Steward Redfrock's intrigues. One by one, Greylock's brothers and cousins had been banished from the High Plateau, until only he survived. But his uncle had grown old, and had ignored his youngest nephew for so long that, for a short time, Greylock had hoped he could frustrate the Steward's schemes, and escape the fate the other members of the royal family had suffered. Then, one day, he too had dared to raise his voice in protest against the foolish teachings of the Gatekeepers, as had his three brothers before him. Too late, he had noticed the presence of his uncle's Steward hovering in the doorway.

Greylock could still summon the awesome scene that had passed before him that morning. He could still see the Steward Redfrock standing behind the throne, bending low, whispering the malicious rumor of his heresy into the Tyrant's ears; could still remember his uncle looking up, searching for him, at last seeing his only nephew across the

11

crowded Court; could still feel within him the fear the Tyrant's icy gaze had created; could still hear his uncle's words ringing in his mind. . . .

"You are not of my family!" the Tyrant had roared. "You are Demon-spawn! I should have destroyed you the same day I discovered the perversion of your mother—and cast you down to the First Tier with her. Begone, Demon! I do not wish to see your kind in my Court again."

Already suffering from his final illness, the Tyrant still had enough spite and strength to rid his kingdom of the last threat from his own blood. Though the old man must have known he was dying, he had exiled the only legitimate claimant to the throne.

His uncle was hopelessly senile, Greylock realized sadly—or why would he have said such things? His mother had died at his birth—so Keyholder had told him, and the old priest had been there! Greylock could only shake his head in dismay at his uncle's foolishness. There would be months of bloodshed when the now hidden rivals emerged to fight for the title of Tyrant; and the ancient tradition of the men of the High Plateau to challenge their Tyrants would make the throne unstable for years to come. The Steward would find that not even his brutal tactics could secure his ambition without a long and bloody struggle.

Greylock knew that Carrell Redfrock would not cease in his efforts to destroy him until the throne, the wealth of the royal family, and—most especially—the Lady Silverfrost, were firmly and finally his. Once the Steward had taken Silverfrost as his wife, his power would be as secure as Greylock's had promised to be. If only Silverfrost had wed me long ago! Greylock thought. He would not have been exiled if he had married the Tyrant's only daughter, no matter what the blasphemy. But she had remained infuriatingly undecided up to the very moment of his exile.

His face flushed in anger as he recalled his leave-taking of her from the icetower of Castle-Guardian, overlooking the green garden of its Icemelt.

"Why do you not do as you are told, Greylock?" she had asked petulantly. "Why must you always do what is forbidden? If you had not been so rebellious—if only I could have been sure of you—we would have married, and this would never have happened." She was idly pulling the red petals of a snowflower and letting them drop onto the fragrant shrubs far below. The petals made their way down through the leaves and fell lightly onto the dark earth, warmed by the volcanic activity beneath the High Plateau.

Greylock reined his impatience and tried once more to explain why he had chosen to journey to the Underworld.

"If I go upward to the Three Peaks, I shall die. I must prove that your father is wrong about the Gateway. If I can find the true course of the path, he will have to take me back. Don't you see that, Silverfrost?"

"Hurry, Greylock!" his sister, Ardra, had hissed from the door of the icetower's uppermost room, where she and Slimspear had stationed themselves nervously to watch for any sign of discovery by the Steward's soldiers.

13

Silverfrost turned from the open window, her light blond hair appearing truly silver as it caught the last rays of moonlight. Her face was uncharacteristically serious.

"You should trust in the gods, Greylock. Just this once, you should place your faith in them. If you did not doubt them so, Father would not have exiled you."

"You know I do not believe there is anything on the peaks of Godshome but the frozen bodies of other exiles; all of them blameless—sent there by the schemes of Carrell Redfrock. I intend to return and fight him, Silverfrost! But you must promise me that you will have nothing to do with him until I return. He is evil!"

"You know that I loathe him!" There was no mistaking the hate in her voice. By now, the first rays of sunlight were glinting off the white snows of the plateau and into the window of the icetower, already raising cold sweat from its walls.

"They are coming!" Slimspear shouted, and at the same moment Greylock heard the sounds of soldiers rushing up the icy steps notched into the tower. Four of the Steward's men burst into the tower room, bowling over the rotund shape of Slimspear, and rushed toward Greylock. The first soldier was impaled on his long royal knife, and in the stunned confusion that followed, Greylock shouted a hasty farewell to his sister and friend, thrust on his Talons, and leaped through the window, catching at the ice with the sharp claws to break his fall.

Luckily, Castle-Guardian, the snowcastle of his friend Slimspear's family, was perched on one corner of the huge glacial plateau that nestled between the Three Peaks of Godshome, looming over the tattered remnant of the trail called the Gateway. Since his route of escape was so near and unexpected, Greylock was able to leave the High Plateau without further challenge.

Suddenly, Greylock tripped over some loose rubble on the path, and almost pitched out over the steep cliff that bordered his road. Brought back to the present by this dangerous stumble, he watched his step carefully. The treacherous mountain trail was seldom used, and in places had crumbled away altogether. At its widest, the trail was no more than a few yards across, and at its most narrow there was no trail at all. Finally Greylock was forced to use his Talons—the slivers of animal horn with which the men of the High Plateau could grip the sheer and frozen sides of cliffs.

At first the sweet full air of the lower elevations had been like nectar to his spirits, adding spring to his step and a broad, brave smile to his face. Now the heat began to raise the sweat on his body, and the thicker air threatened to burst his lungs. His tread became heavy, firm, as if he could only by this solid step convince himself that he could go on. As it grew warmer—unnaturally hot, his senses told him—he kept his eyes open warily for any sign of demons.

He was by now within the layer of clouds which always carpeted the High Plateau, hiding the Underworld, and all he could see was a few feet of gray rock, glistening with moisture. He was relieved that he had not discarded his outer garments, in spite of what he considered an unbearable temperature. At any moment now the snows would begin to fall.

But the moisture he had detected never turned white, but instead began to fall as a thick, cloying rain. Greylock was confused by the wet droplets. Never before had he been below the snowline, and this soaking rain was more disconcerting to him than anything he had yet faced! Even in midsummer, the clouds dropped only snow or ice on the High Plateau; never in memory had the temperature risen above freezing.

Suddenly—unexpectedly—he heard voices ahead. He stopped and peered fearfully into the murk. Demons! he thought, and just as quickly he was disgusted with his superstitious reaction. He didn't even believe in demons! He must control this foolishness! At these stern thoughts, the voices disappeared, confirming to Greylock that his fears were creating imaginary enemies. When he continued, he was purposefully striving to subdue his fears, and he stupidly, almost disastrously, failed to guard the trail behind him. Four soldiers, wearing the black crow insignia of the Steward, and moving with nervous and stealthy speed down the mountain path, were able to surprise him completely.

One of the soldiers could not keep from bellowing a shout of triumph at the sight of their prey, and only this warned Greylock in time. He whirled around, knife in hand just in time to deflect the first blow. He followed this parry with a stab under the extended arm of the soldier, who was pinned with a shocked look against the rock of the cliff. Then the other three soldiers were on him, and he went down heavily in a swirl of arms and legs. Greylock kicked out strongly, and connected. One of the attackers rolled over the cliff, and Greylock could hear his Talons scratch twice—and then heard the man scream as the claws failed to catch. To his dismay he saw the Steward's pet, a huge black mountain crow, fluttering onto the trail above them. The bird watched the fight from a safe distance, smoothing its feathers fastidiously. Greylock briefly wondered how much the bird understood, and for the first time he even wondered if the shiny black bird could somehow communicate with its master.

Suddenly, Greylock realized that they did not mean to kill him at all, but were seeking to capture him. Perhaps the Tyrant has changed his mind, he thought wildly. Far more likely, the Steward Redfrock wished to witness his rival's death personally, and had sent his noisome pet to oversee the capture.

Again Greylock thought he could hear voices drifting up the trail, even from beneath the heaving bodies and muffled grunts of his captors, and he cursed his mind for playing tricks on him at such a time. He was already attributing intelligence to that bird; now he was hearing demons!

This time the soldiers also seemed to hear the sounds, and Greylock found himself struggling with men who were frozen with fear. Suddenly they released him, getting to their feet hastily, ready at that moment to face even the wrath of the Steward Redfrock rather than confront demons. Greylock also rose, at first wary and confused by his sudden freedom, but he quickly saw that the soldiers were not even paying attention to him. Instead they were peering fearfully into the thick fog. Even the crow had cocked its head at the unexpected sounds.

"Demons!" Greylock hissed, and the soldiers were gone, vanishing into the concealing safety of the clouds. The crow cawed once as it hopped nimbly out of the way of the retreating men, but it remained. Greylock thought with a smile that they would probably not stop running until they were safely behind the massive white walls of the snowcastles of the High Plateau. He threw a rock after them, attempting in the same throw to hit the crow. But the crow dodged the stone, and remained poised to take off at the slightest threat from anything other than Greylock.

Greylock turned with grim determination toward the sounds. If he could not go up, then he would have to face the owners of those ghostly voices! Listening carefully, he found that the accents were strange, but except for a few words, he could understand them. There were at least two people from the sounds of the voices, an old man and a young girl. The girl was chastising her companion unmercifully.

"I shall never listen to you again, Grandfather," she was saying. "You promised me that there is Glyden on this mountain. You said it was just lying around waiting to be picked up. You swore that if we did not find any we would return home. Well, where is it?"

"There *is* Glyden, my dear," a mild voice answered. "We just have to go a little higher."

"If we keep going any higher, we shall be

joining these gods of Godshome the Townsmen were speaking of. I'm not ready to join the gods, Grandfather! I will not go any higher until we have found some of this Glyden that is supposed to be so abundant.''

"The Townsmen also spoke of Glyden, Mara. They promised me that there is a Room of Glyden near the top of this trail!''

"And you believed them?'' she snorted. "Why don't they come up and get it themselves? I will never forgive myself for following you on another one of your wild chases for Glyden. It is the last time; you can be sure of that!''

"Just a little higher, Mara.''

"No!''

"Well, at least you could block the wind a little, couldn't you? Are you a Wind-Witch or not? After all, I have contributed the fire.''

"You would be lost without your fire-magic, Grandfather.'' The girl was not hiding her disgust. "I don't ever intend to so depend on my magic. The powers of the wind and fire were never meant for the trivial purposes to which you put them!''

The voices continued to argue, but Greylock was satisfied at last that the owners of these two quarrelling voices could not be demons, and he was strangely certain that they would pose no threat to him. Nevertheless, to be safe he drew his knife before advancing cautiously down the trail. The crow hopped curiously after him, but he ignored it.

The clouds seemed to part reluctantly from the trail, inch by inch, until they were hovering finally about his head. The two strangers he had overheard were crouched over a small fire, set next to a crude wagon which spanned the trail. Greylock saw a blue flame nakedly burning in the cupped palms of the man's hands, yet he could feel the fire's heat even from the distance he kept between himself and the two strangers.

Beyond this peculiar couple, Greylock was met by the sight of mile upon mile of green valleys and winding blue rivers stretching in every direction, a wondrous contrast to his white land of snowcastles. He was astounded by the colors, the growth, the free-flowing waters. So this was the Underworld that the Gatekeepers spoke of in such contempt! He would never have imagined such a beautiful vista as this!

If the effect of his sudden emergence from the clouds was astonishing to him, it was even more so to the two strangers crouched on the trail. To them it appeared as if Greylock had stepped out of the sky, a vision slowly materializing until only his head was still wreathed in the white gossamer of the clouds. On his arms, appearing as a natural extension of his hands, were the sharp claws of his Talons. As he was slowly unshrouded, the young girl, with her mind still on the gods waiting for them in the mountains above, imagined the worst and screamed.

The old man's eyes widened and he stepped back in astonishment. He stumbled against the little cart he had been pushing, and it went over the side of the narrow trail. For a few seconds the old man tried to keep his balance, but then the huge crow—which Greylock had forgotten in his wonder at the Underworld's unveiling— inexplicably flew at the stranger, its claws digging at his face. The blue flame in his hands winked out as the old man protected himself, and he toppled over the cliff after the crashing cart.

Without thinking, Greylock jumped over the side of the cliff after him. He reached instinctively with his talons for cracks he could only hope were there. But his skill in climbing was such that he easily found the few holds that existed in the rock face, and solidly planted his Talons to stop his slide. Then he hurried down to where the old man clung desperately to the mountainside.

The stranger had slid twenty feet down the side of the pass before he had caught precariously at the hardy scrub brush that lined even the steepest of the slopes, wedged into every open crack in the mountainside. But the roots were dangerously shallow and the brush was slowly giving way to the old man's weight. He was in danger at any moment of sliding further down the steep slope, which ended in a sheer drop.

Greylock reached down with one arm while digging in with his Talons, and grasped the desperate man's wrist, knowing that he was probably causing the stranger pain, but hoping that the strength of his grip would also reassure him. He grabbed the man further by the back of his neck and dragged him, not gently, up to safety. Within a few minutes, the two men had crawled exhausted and covered with scratches over the lip of the trail. The old man fell into the waiting arms of the girl, glancing around him fearfully.

"Have you been hurt, Grandfather? That awful raven is gone now."

"Hush, girl!" the old man replied, as if the fall had never taken place. "Why did you scream? He is only a man, as anyone can see!"

"Grandfather!" she repeated, but this time in anger, not concern. "At least you could show gratitude to this stranger for saving your life."

"Yes, I have never seen such climbing!"

Greylock shrugged away the girl's thanks, and the amazement the man expressed at his feat of climbing. How could he tell them that he had always had an affinity for the rocks and stones of the mountains. He did not deserve praise for this commonplace skill.

The two strangers and Greylock stood back now and examined each other openly. That the girl had mistaken him for a god was understandable, for Greylock was as tall and as handsome as any picture of a god she had ever seen. His black curly hair fell about his shoulders, and despite the cold, his chest was bare. He was not heavy, but finely muscled, and he moved with quickness and grace, as they had just witnessed. The only feature that marred his aspect was a thick lock of gray hair which fell over his forehead, though he could not yet have reached his twentieth year. Right now, he was staring back with startled black eyes.

Most of this gaze was reserved for the other man. Greylock could not understand how a man this old could still be living! On the High Plateau such a man would long ago have sought the comfort of the gods before it was too late, or he was too enfeebled to reach the heights. Surely this man was on his way to Godshome now, and therefore could demand of Greylock whatever help and assistance he needed! The old man must be near death, Greylock thought, for the skin was drawn tight about his face and speckled with brown spots. Only the mass of brown hair belied for a moment Greylock's impression of great age, but then the man's severely deformed back obviously showed that he was very old.

He paid little attention to the girl during the first, brief scrutiny. That she was blond and green-eyed, and had reached an awkward age between child and woman was all he noticed. Obviously she had shot up in height recently, and she needed much more weight on her bones to be pretty.

"Who are you?" he finally demanded of them. "What are you doing down here?"

"Why are we *down* here?" the old man seemed startled by this unexpected question. "My name is Moag, a wandering conjuror of fire-magic. And this is my granddaughter, Mara, who also serves as my assistant. But I think before we answer any more questions, we should ask who *you* are, and why you are up here!"

Greylock was satisfied by their words and manner that this strange duo of conjurors were not Carrell Redfrock's spies. But then why were they here? Could they truly have journeyed from the Underworld? He was astonished to find any people on the trail at all, despite his claims of openmindedness. Only now was his mind beginning to play with the startling idea that they had not come from the High Plateau.

"I am Prince Greylock," he said grandly. "I come from above the clouds, from a land of snow-castles and icetowers. I have been banished by my uncle, who is Tyrant of the High Plateau, and I seek the source of the Gateway.'' He could see from their amazed reactions that they were as surprised by his origin as he was of their existence. ''Now, why have you come to the Gateway?''

The old man hesitated, but then greed got the better of his caution. ''We have come in search of Glyden.''

''What is Glyden?'' It was one of the few words he had not understood.

''What is Glyden?'' Moag exclaimed, not bothering to hide his disappointment; but the girl did not seem at all surprised.

''I *told* you there was no Glyden, Grandfather.''

''Hush, Granddaughter. Perhaps he has a different name for it.'' A crafty, hopeful look had entered the wizard's eyes. ''It is a heavy, yellow metal, easily melted and malleable. Do you know of any in these mountains?''

By now Greylock was convinced that these two strangers had indeed emerged from the Underworld, where there should have been only demons. Perhaps no other citizen of the High Plateau, he thought, even Carrell Redfrock, would have been open to such an idea; but Greylock had entertained such ideas since childhood. For the first time he began to hope that there might be a future for him beyond the High Plateau after all. But he would need these two strangers to help him survive the Underworld, at least at first. How could he convince them to accompany him?

From the old man's description of ''Glyden,'' Greylock was fairly certain that he knew of what metal they were speaking. He had to suppress a

24

smile at the wizard's naked greed, as Moag waited for an answer from the man from the land of snow-castles. Obviously, this "Glyden" they spoke of had great value in the Underworld. Perhaps he could use this greed to his own advantage, Greylock thought.

"A yellow metal?" he asked, letting a naive bafflement cross his features. Then he allowed the hilt of his royal knife to be shown. "A metal such as this?"

The old magician almost leaped forward in his eagerness, but Greylock immediately shifted the knife back so that its long blade was facing forward again. Moag stopped at the sight of the gleaming steel.

"Yes, *that* is Glyden," he exclaimed uneasily. "I have promised my granddaughter that I would find her some nuggets for a ring. A worthless metal, of course, but it makes very nice trinkets. Where did you find it?"

Again Greylock had to suppress a smile at the wizard's transparent questions. "Why, Glyden is quite common on the High Plateau! As you say, it is handy for jewelry. We also use it to decorate our buildings—for roofs, and streets, and such."

Which was not quite true of course. Only the Tyrant and his family possessed Glyden, and even then it was used only for jewelry and weapons. Castle-Tyrant, the largest and most ornate of the snowcastles, had some etchings of Glyden on the inner walls, but that was all. No one knew where the metal had come from. Legends placed it in a "Room of Aurim" somewhere along the Gateway—of which the pitiful mountain trail they were now on was the lower reaches. The story Greylock had overheard the wizard tell earlier would not help the old man in his search—it was a tale which every child of the High Plateau knew and nurtured, in hopes of finding the "Room of Aurim." No trace of the metal had been found in its natural state.

Yet there was no denying the existence of the precious metal. It was far more valuable on the High Plateau than Greylock hinted; but judging from the wizard's reactions, not quite as valuable as it was in the Underworld.

The wizard Moag cleared his throat and glanced quickly at his granddaughter, who was still staring at the handsome stranger in amazement.

After leaving the last of the minor fiefdom of Trold, the wizard and his granddaughter had imagined that they were nearing the very ends of the world in their search for Glyden. The names of the lands they had passed through reflected this common belief of the Underworlders. First there had been Far Valley, with its BorderKeep nestled within. Then the endless-seeming, never-changing Twilight Dells. And finally the mountains themselves, dominated by the three spires of Godshome, their white tops barely visible from a great distance. Beyond that, no one they had questioned could say—or seemed to care. But the lure of Glyden and the many legends of its abundance had drawn the wizard halfway across the known world, and into the unknown. He would not stop now, just because of a lack of maps! So it was easy for Moag to believe a stranger's incredible story of riches, of a land where the houses were built of

Glyden. After all, it was what he had come to hear.

"I thank you for your information, Greylock. We will not forget your kindness." Moag motioned for Mara to move along with an urgent wave of his hand from behind his back. "But we must be on our way. I have kept my granddaughter waiting for her ring of Glyden much too long. We'll just visit your land of snowcastles and ice-towers for a little while, and perhaps pick up a few nuggets. Not enough for anyone to notice, of course." He said this in a rush, all the while trying to angle unobtrusively past Greylock.

But Greylock could not let them pass so easily, and quickly gave out the last piece of his hasty scheme. "Surely you do not mean to enter the High Plateau! They would consider you demons, of course." Recalling all the horrid legends of the Underworld, he chose the worst of them. "Did you know that they kill demons—then eat them?"

This last was a wild exaggeration, borrowed from the most horrible of stories about demons; but Greylock thought it likely that any strangers to the High Plateau would be instantly killed, on the assumption that they were demons.

"Eaten?" Moag finally managed to sputter, and for a few moments Greylock did not think his story would be believed. Then Moag fell silent, and he seemed to be weighing the risks. Glyden must be a great temptation indeed, Greylock thought, for the old man to even consider the risk of being devoured!

Suddenly, however, it was the girl who seemed to have grown suspicious. She had stood back and watched the conversation with narrowed eyes.

Now she asked, "You say Glyden is a common material where you come from, Greylock. Yet you, by your own account a prince, have a royal knife encrusted with this valueless metal."

"Yes, it is true," Greylock said with a tone of regret. "I am in disgrace in my uncle's eyes. I was fortunate to have been allowed a weapon at all."

"Why are you bruised and bleeding? Have you been in a fight?" She barraged him with questions, while he tried desperately to think of an answer that would be believable.

"I must have cut myself sliding after your grandfather."

"Where did that raven come from? Was it a pet of yours?" she demanded.

"Hush, Mara! Quit pestering him!" The old man had ended his gloomy reverie, to Greylock's relief, just in time to forestall more embarrassing questions from the girl. Now he was looking at Greylock speculatively. "You say that you are the Tyrant's nephew. Would you also be the heir?"

This was the kind of question Greylock had wanted. "So I would have been. But my uncle grows unfortunately senile, and banished his own heir."

"Your uncle is very old then?"

Greylock nodded.

"Well, Granddaughter," the wizard said heartily. "You must restrain your impatience for a ring of Glyden a little while longer. We must help this young man gain his rightful throne, which he has been so unfairly denied by the capricious whims of an old Tyrant. We must help each other, Prince Greylock! I have some influence in the

28

world below." Mara snorted at this, and the wizard glared at her sternly. "I shall get the help we need!"

"Do not tell me of the capricious whims of an old Tyrant!" Mara said scornfully. "And quit pretending that it is *I* who wants Glyden, Grandfather! You are not fooling anyone. If you are going to be taken in by another wild story of Glyden, then I cannot stop you!"

The girl's admonition prompted Greylock to look at her closely for the first time. Her blond hair had once again fallen into her eyes. She was constantly brushing her locks aside, he had already noticed, with a quick, impatient flick of her hand. Her eyes narrowed at every movement, and she seemed to scrutinize every word that was said. Though she was many years the younger, she seemed by her manner to be the older of the pair—that is, if age could be measured by suspicion.

Greylock sensed that the time would soon come when he would no longer be able to read the old man so well, or see through his blandishments. He guessed that if he had not overheard them on the trail, he would be doubting the wizard's motivations even now. Greylock decided then that he would have to keep a close watch on the girl's suspicious but open expression instead—to keep a semblance of honesty in the new relationship.

"Well, Prince Greylock?" the wizard repeated. "Shall we be partners? All that I will ask of you is that you reward me for my help with a small measure of Glyden."

"It will not be easy, Moag," Greylock felt he

should warn them of the danger they faced. He had lied enough. "It will take an army to enter the High Plateau from the Underworld. A very large army indeed if we wish to wrest Glyden from my uncle's kingdom. My people would fight what they consider 'demons' to the death."

Moag seemed eager to agree, despite the warning. "If we need an army, then we must journey to the fiefdoms of Trold! I know King Kasid personally." Again, the wizard glared warningly at Mara.

"Above all, I must command this army," Greylock continued to lay down his conditions. "The people of the High Plateau would never accept the rule of an Underworlder. No other exile has ever returned before—the snows have claimed them all—so I do not know what my reception will be. But perhaps by the time such an army has been mustered, I will have found the evidence I need to convince the Tyrant, and such a force will not be needed against the Steward. Perhaps. . . ."

"I am certain that King Kasid will help—for a price."

"Very well," Greylock said, at the same time surprised to find within himself the same cunning he had so often seen in his uncle. "Let us be partners then!" Whether or not the old wizard could actually fetch an army was doubtful, Greylock thought. But at least he would have Moag to guide him for the first part of his journey through the Underworld.

Suddenly, Greylock felt the urgency to hurry off the mountain, but without letting them know that they might be pursued. The soldiers would have returned by now, and Steward Redfrock would have been told that his enemy was still alive. At any moment now, another, more determined sortie of soldiers would be coming after him. And if the crow had gotten back sooner, and had somehow communicated what had happened, then this dawdling on the trail could be disastrous.

"I feel a storm coming," he lied, explaining that the people of the High Plateau could always feel a change in the weather. "We had better hurry off this exposed path."

Mara looked at him, suspicious of the sudden urgency in his voice, once again eyeing his bruises and obviously feeling that her grandfather was committing them to a dangerous partnership. But she followed Greylock without a word, for she too felt exposed on the high mountain trail.

● ● ●

Carrell Redfrock was at that moment angrily dismissing the two soldiers who had come back to report their failure. He made a mental note to find a proper punishment for them, but most of his rage had already dissipated. His Familiar, the black crow that the people of the High Plateau foolishly believed was a simple pet, had related what had happened minutes ago. Unfortunately, the Familiar had not stayed to see if Greylock was able to save the old man. But the Steward knew Greylock's climbing abilities well, and did not doubt he would succeed in retrieving the stranger.

Redfrock could not help but wonder at the coincidence that had placed two Underworlders on the

Gateway at the same moment that Prince Greylock descended. Only he knew how unlikely that was, for Greylock was wrong when he believed himself the only person of the High Plateau capable of going down from Godshome. The Steward Redfrock had made the trip several times long ago, in his search of methods to overthrow the Tyrant. He had come back with his Familiar—and the knowledge of powerful allies in the Underworld.

Redfrock berated himself for not considering the Gateway as an escape route for Prince Greylock. The youth had made his opinions well known. But the Steward had not believed Greylock would have the courage to face demons. Now, he had two reasons for making sure that his rival was dead. As long as the prince was alive he was a threat to the Steward's plans. But even more important, Greylock was now a threat to his Master.

It had been made clear to Redfrock that no one was to discover the true location of the Gateway, and for this reason the Steward had encouraged the superstitions of the mountain people. Now Greylock was very close to the truth, without realizing it. There was only one thing to do: he must send a party after Greylock. The youth must never discover the true entrance to Gateway, and the easiest way to accomplish this was to remove him from the Tiers of Existence.

He called back the two disgraced soldiers, who entered the room chastened and servile. "Gather a company of two dozen men, and go after Prince Greylock. I want him dead, and I do not want you to come back until that has been done. I do not care if you have to cross half of the Underworld—

32

I want him dead!''

The two soldiers blanched, but immediately saluted and started to leave.

''No, wait!'' he changed his mind rapidly. ''I think I will have to lead this expedition myself. The Tyrant is already regretting his action. If Greylock should ever return, the Tyrant might even welcome him. I must be sure that never happens. Now go! We shall leave in the morning. One of you tell the Lady Silverfrost that I wish to have dinner with her tonight.''

One of the soldiers hesitated, and the Steward demanded, ''Well? What is it?''

''The Lady Silverfrost has already received your invitation, Steward. She . . . refuses to come.''

''She refuses to eat dinner with me?'' Redfrock was incredulous. ''I must believe that you did not ask her properly. Now go back and ask her again. Tell her it is my *wish* that she come to dinner—tonight!''

After the two soldiers had left hastily, the Steward smiled and turned, crooking a finger at the crow, which was perched on a dead trunk of a tree installed in the corner of his icetower. The Castle-Steward had the smallest of the High Plateau's Icemelts, but Redfrock did not mind. He had never cared for greenery, and he shuddered at the thought of descending into the Underworld again. He had no power over the denizens of the Underworld and he always felt vulnerable in its humid growth.

The crow jumped onto his shoulder and he began absently feeding it meaty scraps. Carrell Redfrock appeared slender and frail, and almost as old as the Tyrant—and he cultivated this image. For beneath his scarlet robes, the Steward was wiry and strong, and far from old. His carefully thinned white hair was swept back from his forehead, displaying his bushy white eyebrows and craggy features.

He maneuvered the crow to his gauntleted right hand. "Tell our friend in the BorderKeep that I am coming down from Godshome. If I do not contact him again, he should watch for a stranger with a lock of gray hair. He is to agree to everything this stranger asks. Is that understood?"

The black eyes of the crow seemed to stare back for a moment, and then the bird rose with the Steward's hand and launched itself noisily through the window of the icetower, where it was quickly lost in the night.

Chapter Two

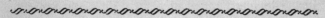

Greylock concealed from his new partners the fear he felt when the trio began to descend into the bright sunlight of the Underworld. It would not do for them to see that he was frightened of mere legends and superstition. They had already laughed heartily at his descriptions of grotesque ghouls, just as he had laughed at the horrible beings they had imagined lay in wait for them on Godshome.

Despite his own skepticism, and their reassurances, Greylock kept a wary eye open for demons, and his hands never strayed far from the Glyden hilt of his knife. He doubted, however, that any of his people would follow him this far down the mountain, even under the Steward Redfrock's dire threats. At least he was safe from that!

Greylock noticed that the wizard's covetous eyes rarely strayed from the gleaming Glyden for very long, and he even wondered briefly if he would be able to trust the old man not to club him on the head when he wasn't looking. He began to suspect that there was more than greed in Moag's looks of longing.

Little by little Greylock discarded most of his thick mountain garments, until he was left with a thin robe—and he was still sweating heavily beneath that light cloth. His new partners remained heavily bundled well into—what seemed to Greylock, at least—the hot and steaming foot-hills. The sharp claws of his Talons hung loosely from the hide straps tied to his wrists, to be taken up in his grip whenever the trail became too rough and the Underworlders needed his help to get by the sudden gaps.

This became less and less necessary as the trail finally broadened near the bottom of the pass, and their progress speeded. He began to watch for any sign of the rubble and rusted iron that might indicate the ruins of Gateway's giant portals. He thought it unlikely that there was a gate at all—only a figurative closure from the Underworld, never opened until now. But he had doubts.

It was difficult to believe, for instance, that the narrow and treacherous trail they were now traversing, so long unused, opened near the upper reaches of the pass into a wide, magnificent roadway. It was this road, with its mammoth stones and intricate patterns, that had succeeded in raising doubt in Greylock's mind, and had kept him from discounting the ancient legends entirely. It was this remnant of the Gateway that the Gatekeepers were pledged to protect and maintain. Yet the road led nowhere, ending in the desolate snows of Godshome. Everyone knew that the Third Holy Tier contained nothing but the falling snows and howling winds of nature, and none had ever returned to tell of "gods." Greylock's mistake had been to say aloud that the passage of time had distorted the true meaning of Gateway, and it was this heresy that had finally given the Steward Redfrock the opportunity to disgrace Greylock in the eyes of the Tyrant. But if he could prove he was right, and that there was more to Gateway than this unused pathway, then his uncle would have to take him back, and allow him to wed Silverfrost.

The boundary between the mountains and the Underworld was clear, at least to Greylock. The ground seemed somehow tainted to him. It seemed as if he were stepping from a robust and cruel land to a sickly and even crueler land. Something within him, something that had never before been touched, was offended by the light loam earth, and he hesitated before he stepped onto it. The first few steps brought a violent shudder; a strange revulsion at the feel of the brown dirt beneath his feet. Greylock followed the wizard and the girl only because they appeared to be unaffected by it. Indeed, they didn't even seem to notice that this land was different, decaying.

Greylock could see layer upon layer of the emerald green valleys, and rounded foothills seemingly perched on top of each other, wreathed in swirling mists. The light appeared to grow dim, as if the sun had suddenly gone behind a cloud. Yet when Greylock glanced up, the shimmering globe of the sun still filled the sky. The heat grew even more intense, despite the darkness, and the unfamiliar itching discomfort of his sweat made him miserable. He was irritated when the other two travelers moaned their appreciation of the heat.

On a stone ledge overlooking a river that ribboned back and forth down the last of the steep slopes, Moag warned Greylock of the dangerous lands they were now entering. The wizard explained how the two had fallen on hard times in the Twilight Dells.

"I depend on the patronage of rulers and landowners," he said. "I do their bidding with my magic and they reward me with their Glyden. But in this land there are no rulers, no rich men. Each house is a stronghold for a small clan, and they jealously guard their own worthless territories, though each valley is small, poor, and infertile. I do not understand why they have not left this country long ago. This earth will yield no more!"

Old man Moag shuddered. "I have not eaten well or slept well since I entered this accursed land! We will find no armies among the Wyrrs. We must go beyond the Twilight Dells, beyond even the BorderKeep—to the glorious fiefdoms of Trold, my homeland! Let us travel as fast as we can through this country, for only death lies in its valleys."

Greylock realized that what the old man had just said explained his own uneasiness at entering this new country. But how had he known that the land was ill? It looked no different than any other land, the little he had seen of the Underworld.

Yet he did not raise this perplexing question, to his later regret, for he never suspected that it would concern him. Instead, he was much more interested in what he thought the wizard had just revealed. Greylock believed he had detected in the old man's words the real motivations for his greed—more, perhaps, than Moag may have wished. He eyed the mage's tattered garments doubtfully. "If the Kings of Trold would pay you in Glyden, then why did you not stay in Trold and earn their reward?"

"It is their Glyden, not mine," the wizard growled, his tone indicating that he did not like these prying questions. "The Glyden is never mine—it is the wages of a servant, and I do not wish to be a servant any longer."

"But if you are a magician, why do you not just summon the wealth you wish?"

"There are two things a wizard cannot conjure, and those are money and food. Nor may he conjure up anything for just himself. And he must be paid in Glyden for his services; only then is his magic released, to serve that person. Yet at the end of his service, he must give it all back! That is why the wizard is always under the domination of others; why he must always serve the rich."

So this was the reason for the wizard's single-minded obsession with Glyden! Greylock could see that the whole arrangement had obviously soured the old man, and it seemed Moag would be willing to travel anywhere and do anything to possess his own Glyden—for Glyden meant freedom.

"If only Mara and I had our own wealth!" the

39

old man wailed. "A simple trade and we would be free. I would never have to serve another stranger again."

Mara, as usual, had the last word. "Of course, it never occurs to Grandfather that he might earn Glyden by some honest labor—say with his hands!"

Greylock soon learned that crossing this land of hills and sudden dales would not be easy. It was more a maze than a road, he thought, for they could not just cross any valley they wished, moving in a straight line that might reasonably have brought them to an end of the land. Instead they were forced to follow a winding course; halfway down one valley, only to retreat and move at right angles, and so on in an incomprehensible way, until Greylock was at last hopelessly lost, and dependent on the wizard completely to guide them out of this nightmare land.

Moag had apparently learned from bitter experience which valleys would prove friendly, or at least safe, and which were dangerous. "If I had not already traveled through this land," the old man said darkly, "it would take us a very long time to cross. But even now we must be careful. If we turn into the wrong valley we could be set upon and beaten. Or perhaps even killed. We must hurry to set our camp in a safe place, for it is in the dark hours that the Wyrrs truly have power we need fear."

So far the mage must be choosing correctly, Greylock thought, for they had yet to see any of the inhabitants of this land of constant evening, friendly or unfriendly.

"Where are they, old man? Hiding?"

"They are actually more frightened of us than we are of them," Moag explained. "Some great ill has crossed this land, setting neighbor against neighbor. Though each valley alone can afford only a poor existence, they never leave their own valleys as far as I know. I gathered from my inquiries at the BorderKeep that, just a few years ago, surviving such a trip as we are now on would have been unthinkable. But it seems that the natural human spirit is reasserting itself, and time is wearing away their fear. The Wyrrs are not as murderous as they once were, though there are still pockets. . . ."

"Why are they afraid?" Greylock asked, somehow moved by the plight of the Wyrrs.

"They do not say. I believe their crime was so dire that, whatever it was, they will never tell. Sometimes they seem to be watching, as if they are waiting for somebody. Perhaps that is why they no longer murder every stranger who steps into the Twilight Dells."

The three visitors moved carefully through valley after valley, each one seeming more silent and eerie than the last. Soon Greylock had the disquieting sense of being watched—but Moag hushed him quickly when he mentioned this.

"Put away your Talons, Prince Greylock. They look too much like a weapon. We do not want to provoke the Wyrrs."

"Are we not to fight if we are attacked?"

"Perhaps not. You must let me decide. Only if our lives are in danger will you need to fight. They may just wish to taunt us."

41

"But how will you know?" Greylock had already decided he would fight.

"I may not!" the wizard answered cryptically and would not explain his answer. The old man's hunched back bobbed up and down in front of Greylock's eyes, forbidding any more questions.

Greylock compared what the old man had just told him to the legends in his own land about the Underworld, and was startled to see the similarities. Indeed, it did seem as if each "demon" was caged, only to strike out in murderous anger at interlopers. Despite the danger, Greylock almost wished that some of the strange natives of this land would show themselves. If what the old man had heard was true, it was no wonder that no one had emerged from the Underworld before—and that no one had dared to visit it!

Their torturous route began to seem to Greylock like one of the games of his childhood, when he and his friend Slimspear had explored the hundreds of caverns which served as a kind of highway beneath the snows of the glacier. There they had tried to lose each other by cunning turns. Now the trick was to find a path through adjacent valleys that were safe. Often the wizard would stop and frown and remain unmoving for long minutes of concentration, while Greylock would wait impatiently. Greylock began to suspect that the old man was also lost, but since he had long ago lost his own way, and had only Moag to guide him safely out of the puzzle, he said nothing.

Occasionally they could see the roofs of the Wyrrs' crude dwellings at the ends of the valleys, but Moag was careful not to wander too close to the interiors, and they remained unmolested that first day. The old wizard actually seemed to cheer up as they made camp in one of the few empty dells, near the ruins of an old shack, with its gray wood hanging over them, decaying and moldy.

Before daylight had completely left the valley, Greylock caught Mara staring at him surreptitiously with a wondering look. She turned away quickly at his scowl. For some reason, Greylock was irritated by the girl's constant scrutiny.

"Well?" he demanded. "What is it now?"

To his surprise, she answered him. "Your hair...."

"What about my hair? I have had this gray lock of hair since my fifth year of existence on the Second Tier." Greylock realized with some surprise that it was the first time he had had to explain his distinction since those first years, when he had gotten into fight after fight to defend his wounded honor. The other children had called him an "old man," he remembered, and had teased him with the question of how soon he would ascend to the First Tier. He wondered why it should bother him now. He had long ago proven that he was a match for any man.

"I'm sorry, Prince Greylock. I did not mean to comment, but your hair did not seem so gray when we met you on the mountain trail. It seems to have spread over your scalp. Perhaps the light of the fire is misleading."

Moag turned from his tending of the fire and looked at his partner with some interest for the first time in many miles. "Mara is right, Prince Greylock. Your hair has become more gray since

43

we first met you. Look for yourself!"

With that invitation, the fire behind Moag's back leaped toward the tree limbs high above, and by this magical light Greylock was able to catch a reflection of himself in the wide blade and glowing red handle of his knife. He saw that the lock of gray hair that had always marked him had spread, so that most of the matt of curls which fell over his forehead had turned gray. He was dismayed by the change, for the hair on his head had not changed in color for many years.

"It appears that this land has wrought a change," Moag mused. "Perhaps there have been changes inside of you as well, Prince Greylock."

The next morning the old man led them with uncharacteristic straightforwardness and assurance, but Greylock felt a strange forboding. He was becoming accustomed to this strange land, and somehow uncomfortably attuned to it. The old man was right, the earth was creating a change within him. Often it seemed as if he could sense the presence of Wyrrs before Moag did, and sometimes he could not restrain his impatience when the wizard dawdled, trying to decide by memory and sight whether a valley was safe to enter.

Finally, after another of his long ruminations, the old man made the wrong choice. Greylock could feel that they were approaching a dwelling that was not empty or deserted, but was filled with the odd aura of the Wyrrs. But since Moag was whistling happily, and seemed sure of his route, Greylock did not object.

Suddenly, he saw the wizard looking about him nervously, as if he had just noticed his mistake. At

44

the same moment they were surrounded by scrawny creatures so dirty, pale, and emaciated that they appeared inhuman. What hair they still had, even the youngest of them, was silver gray.

"Demons!" Greylock yelled, even as he realized that they were human, though barely alive. Some of them indeed seemed more dead than alive. Despite the sweltering heat, they were bundled heavily in swaths of cloth that were little more than rags. Yet even through these coverings Greylock could tell that they were bone thin. These people were almost what he had envisioned demons to be like. They made no threatening movements. "I think I may have found demons after all!" he said.

"You may be right, my boy," Moag muttered under his breath balefully. "You may be right. But do not fight them. There are more in this group than I have ever seen together. I will see if I can talk to them."

The wizard stepped forward with his hands showing empty. As if this were a threatening gesture, instead of a sign of peace, the mass of Wyrrs surged toward them with a shrill roar.

Since the Wyrrs were unarmed, Greylock did not draw his weapon, but batted the first attackers away easily with his bare hands. The Wyrrs appeared so weak and ill nourished that Greylock thought he could fight his way out of the trap, if he used his knife. But the magician once again shouted for him not to resist, and he realized that in order to escape he would have to leave his new partners behind. Not admitting to himself that he had grown to like them and would never leave Mara, or even the old man, with the Wyrrs, Greylock told himself that he needed them still to regain Silverfrost and find the course of Gateway. He would trust the wizard this time, he decided. If he was wrong in his trust, it would be the last time—one way or another.

The Wyrrs saw his resolve weakening and attacked him in a mass. His sense of dignity was sorely tried at being overwhelmed by such scrawny specimens of humanity. Their blows hurt his pride even more than his body. Yet, along with his scorn, Greylock felt an inexpressible pity for these people—doomed to live forever in this sad land of twilight.

The three prisoners were led roughly toward one of the huge, primitive structures they had glimpsed earlier through the trees. Greylock realized at a closer look that the building was rather pathetically designed to withstand siege, but only to hold off foes just as weak.

The trespassers were dumped on an uneven dirt floor. The building was just one room, divided, it seemed, by the natural refuse of clan living. In the center was a fire, and smoke found exits through the many cracks in the roof and walls. The structure did not seem to give much shelter, for the hard packed earthen floor was still damp from the rains. Rubbish and badly cured hides lay in piles about the floor. Children were perched silently on the rafters, staring down on them with unnaturally bright and enlarged eyes.

The leader of the Wyrrs, grotesquely tall and thin, had still not said a word, and now the troop retreated back against the walls at his gesture. Of the three captives, they had seemed to be most interested in Greylock, several of them pinching him as if to see if his muscles and fat were real, running their dirty fingers through his gray locks wonderingly, and pulling at his longer dark hair. Greylock suffered this examination without a word, wincing as they probed the muscles of his arms and legs.

"What are they going to do to us, Moag?"

"I believe that they are going to eat us," Moag said gloomily.

"What!" Greylock didn't believe him. "No human would do that to another!"

"Why, Prince Greylock!" Mara said mockingly. "I thought that is what your own people did to strangers! You should not be surprised. At least these people could use the food."

"Of course we don't eat anyone!" Greylock did not think it was a time for humor. "I thought you were barbarians to believe that. But don't feel smug. My uncle would have killed you without another thought."

"We believed you, Prince Greylock, because we had just passed through the real danger of the Twilight Dells!"

The three prisoners glumly watched the huge central fire being stoked, its black smoke curling up through a hundred small holes in the roof. Every once in a while, in spite of himself, Greylock would mutter, "Demons!" Was he about to die discovering that his father and the Gatekeepers were right? It was too much for him to continue his stoic restraint. He would not end being someone's meal! He shuddered and vowed that he would fight his way free if he had to, even if it meant leaving

47

the other two behind. Even with his hands tied, he was a match for these Wyrrs!

The fire's heat was now becoming uncomfortable, and Greylock imagined his gray hair singeing. Mara squirmed beside him, turning first one part of her body and then another to the exposed fire. But the wizard lay quietly on his back, the hunch at his shoulders elevating his head just enough so that he could stare gloomily into the flames near his feet.

"Why did you let them capture us?" Greylock asked him. "Why did you not let me fight them?"

"Do not worry, Prince Greylock. I know a means of escape if nothing else works. But I do not wish to use that way unless I must."

"You had better hurry, Moag," Greylock urged. "Whatever route of escape you choose had best be quick!"

Finally, the magician saw that Greylock was right. The Wyrrs were obviously not going to let them go. "I was hoping I would not have to do this, but there does not seem to be any other way." He looked at Greylock as if it would hurt him woefully to say what he was about to propose. "You must be my patron, Prince Greylock—master of my services. Only then will I be able to use my magic."

"Of course, Moag," Why hadn't the wizard said something before now? "Get on with it! What must I do?"

"You must promise that you will pay me, and take care of my worldly needs as long as I am in your service, which will not be for long."

Greylock was disappointed. "But I have nothing

to give you, Moag! I will share whatever I have...."

"You need not give it all to me now," the wizard said impatiently. "Just promise me the payment, and it will be done."

"I so deed it," he said hastily.

"The payment must be in Glyden, Greylock!" the old man warned. "You must promise that you will give me your knife—that will be adequate."

Greylock hesitated at this condition. "I will get it back?"

"As soon as you release me from your service," Moag assured him. "I have no wish to be your servant, Greylock. You will get it back."

"Then you may have the blade. Now get on with it, Moag! They're just about ready."

"Good," the wizard nodded, satisfied. While these hurried and whispered negotiations had been going on, the Wyrrs had continued to gather along the walls. Finally, all the stealthy movement had stopped, and the prisoners realized with a shock that all the bright eyes of the Wyrrs were on them, and the fire was prepared.

"Now which spell would be best?" Moag mused. "Ah, yes. A simple smoke spell should be sufficient. Keep an eye on the tall Wyrr leader who has your knife, Greylock. You must retrieve it, at all costs!"

"Hurry, old man!" Greylock hissed.

"I have already begun," the wizard said complacently.

At first Greylock could see no results from Moag's vague mumblings. As he waited and watched for something spectacular to happen, the hot fire's smoke seemed to be getting into his eyes. He saw the dim forms of the Wyrrs moving forward to lift him to the fire, and he prepared to fight them with the bulk of his body, if nothing else. When Mara coughed beside him, Greylock finally had his first inkling of what the old man meant to do. The smoke grew thicker—and the black figures of the Wyrrs never reached him. He hurriedly marked the last position of the leader of the Wyrrs, the one who held the Glyden-hilted knife.

The smoke had completely filled the interior, and he felt hands pulling at his bonds. "Quickly, get the knife and let us begone!" he heard the old man's voice say from behind him, though when he turned he could see nothing. He wondered how the wizard had managed to free himself. "You must get the knife!" the voice repeated, and then was gone.

Greylock moved quickly toward the last spot he had seen the tall Wyrr, already masked by the smoke. But it did not prove necessary to search blindly. The Wyrr stumbled into him, his reddened eyes watering and closed, coughing violently. Greylock wondered at this reaction, for the smoke seemed mild to him. Much as he wanted to punish the man, pity suddenly moved him and he merely stripped the man of the weapon and pushed him away.

Yet even this gentle rebuff was too much for the Wyrr. Greylock could hear the air forced from the man's chest when he was pushed, and felt his own hand penetrate deep into the Wyrr's stomach. As the tall man folded up and fell to the ground,

Greylock was left with a squeamish feeling in his hand where it had touched the Wyrr's backbone.

"I have it, Moag!" he shouted, when he had recovered from this shock. "I have the knife!"

Then he was outside somehow, though he could not remember passing through a portal. The smoke seemed just as thick, but he could see the moon shining dully through the fog.

"Greylock!" He heard his name called, and the voice seemed to him to be coming from all sides at once.

Turning and spinning at the echoes, he dared to shout out, "Where are you?" once, hoping that he was not revealing himself to the Wyrrs in the process. His shout seemed to be quickly absorbed by the damp suffocating fog.

"Stay where you are, Greylock!" This time the wizard's voice seemed to be much closer—almost beside him, though he knew that was impossible.

Then he did feel the presence of his two partners, though he could still not see them. The girl's small hand pulled at his and he followed obediently, blindly. Suddenly, they were clear of the fog—or the old man had removed the last of its concealing mantle from them. Greylock looked back to see the fortress, and a hundred yards on all sides of it, bounded in by the clouds of smoke—yet the rest of the clear night sky was lit by the light of a full moon. Occasionally, the muffled form of a Wyrr would emerge, surrounded by his own little cloud, until the thin form would stumble inevitably back into the fog to join the others. Their cries—dismayed, frightened—drifted over to the watchers.

51

Yet Greylock was disappointed with the results. "So that is fire-magic? It is not so much."

"It worked, didn't it?" the mage said crossly. "Never be spectacular if something humble will work just as well, I always say. Now if you will just hand me my payment."

"You'll give it back?"

"Yes, hurry!"

Reluctantly, Greylock pulled the blade from his belt and began to hand it over to the old man.

Moag snatched it from his grasp while it was still several inches away—and Greylock was showing signs of changing his mind. "You must pay me, Prince Greylock. One does not deny the forces of magic."

The wizard stared down at the royal knife and turned it over in his hands, fondling the soft hilt of of Glyden. Then, with an ostentatious show of sacrifice, he proffered it to Greylock. "I have been paid, and now I return the payment for my freedom." He said this almost formally. "Take it, Prince Greylock! Once you take it back it will release me from the agreement, and we can be on our way. I cannot hold the smoke forever, you know."

"Release you from our bargain already?" Greylock asked, confused by the wizard's eagerness to give back the knife. "I thought you wanted Glyden. Perhaps you should hold onto it a while longer. We may have desperate need of your magic."

"I have told you—it is not my Glyden, it is yours. I do not wish to be a servant again, not when I will have to give the Glyden back when

I no longer serve you."

"But what if we should need you again?" Greylock was troubled by their vulnerability in the Twilight Dells, and indeed, in the Underworld. The wizard had just shown that his magic could be most useful.

"Then I will enter your service again!" Moag was beginning to look noticeably worried.

"What if it is too late? Or what if I should lose the knife, and don't have the Glyden you require next time?"

"If you don't release me," the wizard said angrily, "then you must pay me. In Glyden! The only Glyden you have is also your only weapon. Will you give me your weapon or my freedom?"

Greylock paused at this, while the old man looked on smugly at his dilemma. He had not thought of that! Reluctantly, he came to the conclusion that, useful as the wizard's magic could have been, he could not trust the old man with the only weapon among them; not when it was also his heirloom, the only proof he still owned of his royal heritage. If he ever hoped to return to the High Plateau, he would need to hold onto his knife.

Mara saved him from making a painful decision. "Don't release him, Prince Greylock!" she said, and Greylock caught a rare unguarded look from the mage—a cross look that told her to be silent.

Greylock snatched his hand back. "Why?"

"Let him keep the knife. Once in your service, Grandfather can do nothing to harm you. Remember you are now his master. It is as safe with him as it would be with you."

"A nice paradox!" Greylock said.

"You would not hold me against my wishes?" the old man asked in a horrified tone.

"Perhaps I will. For a little while."

"I will not serve you willingly, Prince Greylock," the wizard said furiously. "I will not forget that you have done this to me!"

"But, Moag! You tried to trick me and your trick did not work. Do I not have a right to your services for a little while? I will release you soon, I promise you. As soon as you have learned your lesson. Besides, this is best for us all, don't you see? Now we shall have the use of your magic; and since you lost your packs on the mountain, and I lost mine in the Wyrr's fortress, we shall need magic."

"I curse the day I met your grandmother," the wizard said angrily to Mara. "The women of this family have been nothing but trouble!"

"Careful, Grandfather! Remember, your magic is working now."

The wizard hastily made a sign and muttered, "Forgive me, Mara." Moag was obviously speaking to the grandmother—or perhaps the mother—but not the girl.

Greylock interrupted what he saw might turn into a long argument. "Now, Moag, as you pointed out, we had better be on our way. The smoke seems to be dissipating somewhat."

As they moved hastily from the valley, Greylock was already feeling troubled by his betrayal. But when, at the last moment, the wizard turned and crooked a finger, summoning the cloud of smoke, Greylock once again convinced himself that it was for the best. They had need of the old man's powers. He would let the wizard go as soon as they were out of danger, he told himself.

Soon they were enveloped by the harmless fog, and thus shrouded and concealed, they walked directly east, no longer caring if they encountered Wyrrs or not. None of them said a word. The old man walked stooped over as if he were examining the trail, and Greylock thought he could occasionally hear an angry grumble from the wizard, his mottled face seemingly fixed in a permanent scowl. The girl followed close behind him, seeming tiny and frail between the two men. She too had not said anything since they had left the valley of the Wyrrs, and was apparently also suffering from the guilt of her betrayal. Her frown made it clear to Greylock that she had not done it for him, but had her own reasons. Her smoke-smudged fair face and darkening blond hair seemed to fit her mood. It was obvious that she would not welcome any questions from Greylock. He was last in line, still not certain that they were safe, and feeling naked without a sword.

Once he thought he heard the sounds of fighting behind him, and several times he saw the black shape of a mountain crow flying far overhead. Such birds were common, but Greylock was becoming more and more uncomfortable with his defenselessness. Finally this vulnerability became too much to bear, and he called out for Moag to stop.

"What is it now?" the wizard said crossly.

Despite the old man's glowering countenance Greylock asked his question. "I must have a weapon, Moag. Can your fire-magic make me or summon me, a weapon?''

"I cannot make something out of nothing," the mage growled.

"What would you need?"

The wizard's impatience was becoming increasingly noticeable. Greylock doubted he would have even been answered if it were not for the fact that he was also Moag's master.

"I would need the same ingredients as would be in the weapon itself; metal for metal, stone for stone, wood for wood, and so on; though it need not be in the same proportions."

Greylock looked around at the landscape of small trees, and sharp stones, doubtfully. Then he remembered the last gift of his eldest brother, before he too had been sent away by their uncle's envy and wrath. It was a small jewel-encrusted Glyden replica of their uncle's royal sword, Thunderer—exact in every detail, but only two inches long. Greylock always carried it with him in a small homemade sheath, for the blade actually cut and was useful for little things.

"How about this?" he asked, drawing it forth from his pocket with some difficulty. "Can you do anything with this?"

Despite the wizard's obvious anxiety at having stopped in the middle of the Twilight Dells, he grabbed the little blade and examined it with gleaming eyes. "Why did you not tell me you had this?"

"Does it matter?"

"No, I suppose not." Moag seemed troubled. "You did say that this kind of metal and stone were common in your land."

The wizard turned his attention to the little sword again and nodded. "I may be able to reproduce the steel of the blade itself, but alas, the valuable stones and Glyden are beyond my power, as I have told you. Still, it is better than nothing. "You *should* be armed. Lay it down, with the sheath on it, and turn your eyes."

Greylock placed it upon a rock which was about waist high, and turned to cover his eyes. Even so, the flash that ensued raised stars before his eyes. He turned to see a new Thunderer, still glowing from the intense heat of its creation. Greylock gasped and gingerly felt the warm Glyden of the hilt. He removed the crude sheath with a caressing movement, and the new blade sparkled even in the dim light of the Twilight Dells.

"It is Thunderer!" he said, wonderingly.

The old man sat sprawled upon the path, his legs stuck out in front of him like two knobby branches of a tree—stunned and more than a little confused.

"Something went wrong with the spell!" he said. "It was as if someone took control of the spell and bent it to his own will. I have never felt such power!"

Moag got up slowly, unsteadily, and his eyes focused on the new sword. He seemed completely taken aback by the sight.

"This is not possible! I chanted a simple spell of forging, nothing more." He examined the sword as if he could find an explanation in its surface or a flaw in its work. "This is a better weapon than it should be—better than the laws of magic should have allowed. It cannot be true Glyden. It must be simulated, somehow. Still, I believe we shall be the object of every thief in the hundred fiefdoms of Trold!''

"It is real, Moag. I can feel it."

The wizard shook his head, confused and unable to accept what he was seeing. He was startled by the sword's beauty and aura of power. For the first time, he began to look upon Prince Greylock as someone other than a partner in greed—or an unwanted master. This uncommon deed had not been done for a common man!

Mara was also looking at Greylock with a different look in her bright green eyes. As he strapped on the new blade, fancying the way it slapped against his leg, he smiled gleefully at her. She smiled back shyly.

The smile changed her sullen countenance into the fair and pleasant face her green eyes and blond hair had always promised. Perhaps she was finally believing that he was a prince, he thought, and it somehow pleased him to impress her. She was just a girl compared to the Lady Silverfrost—yet she seemed to have unaccountably gained weight and was more and more appealing.

As they continued, the old man walking ahead of them bent over in thought, Greylock tried to engage her in conversation.

"Why did you help me, Mara?"

"I did not do it for you! I did it for Grandfather, and for myself. I am tired of traveling from place to place, always in search of Glyden and never finding any. It is only when we serve someone that we settle down for a while. But lately Grandfather would rather starve than give in. After this, I'm afraid he will never use his magic

58

for others. He has this dream of finding Glyden, you see." She sighed deeply. "I suppose he thinks we shall hire each other, and therefore be able to care for each other's every need for the rest of our lives."

"But I do not have a home to give you, Mara. I am as poor as you are."

"You *will* have a home, Prince Greylock. Someday you will have a kingdom!" Greylock wondered how she could be so certain. "It is time we found a place to stay," she continued, "and it is better that we serve a Tyrant than a poor farmer who happens to own a small trinket of Glyden. It is better to serve in luxury, after all, than serve in poverty. If we must serve, of course."

"If I ever reclaim my throne, you will be given all you ask!" Greylock vowed fervently.

She looked at him searchingly, her green eyes showing doubt and concern. "You must promise me that you will let my Grandfather go when that happens, Greylock. Let Moag finally have some Glyden of his own, with no price on it."

"Of course!"

They both fell silent at this, troubled by the trick they had played on Moag.

Several times during the rest of that long day, Greylock thought he caught a glimpse of movement behind him, but since it was still far away he assumed that the Wyrrs were stalking them from a safe distance.

The Twilight Dells seemed never changing; never fully light, never fully dark. When night fell, and they sat around a fire, it did not seem as if a full day had passed in all the time they had been traveling. Yet it seemed as if they had always been traveling. Though Moag grumbled at the loss of his cart, he seemed to be able to do most things by magic. Greylock watched the wizard light a fire in the rain with damp wood.

"Can you teach me some of this fire-magic?" he asked curiously.

"Don't bother to learn it, Greylock," Mara said in disgust. "Magic is nothing you cannot already do by hand, if you are willing to work a little."

"My granddaughter could learn," Moag said, ignoring her comment. "It is in her blood but she doesn't want to. I suspect that she already knows a great deal, however. I am almost certain she is a Wind-Witch, though she denies it. She refuses to use her wind-magic, for she confuses all magic with the admittedly flawed characters of her father and grandfather. It is such a waste of talent!"

"But what about me?" Greylock persisted. "Could I learn?"

"You would already know if you could," Moag answered simply. "For instance, I am a Fire-Wizard. I have always had power over the flames. My granddaughter, I suspect, is a Wind-Witch, as I have said. There are also Earth-Wizards, and Water-Witches, and so on. We all have some small measure of power over the other elements, but the power is usually concentrated in one of the four elements; earth, fire, wind, and water."

Greylock asked no more questions of the old man, but he wondered as he prepared for bed if Moag could be wrong. On the High Plateau magic was not known, yet there were often phenomena that were unaccounted for. In his family, for instance, there was an instinctive feel of the land. On the High Plateau, a youth would not necessarily know if he possessed power over any of the elements. He might realize that such an element responded well to his touch, but if he had not been trained, if he did not know it was possible, that power might remain undeveloped. It was not like the wizard's own family, which by his own account, had had generations of magicians.

He wondered briefly if he should tell the wizard of his revulsion to the land, now stronger than ever as he prepared to lie upon it for a night's sleep. But he knew the old man would just dismiss the vague feeling as imagination.

There was one thing the old man's magic could not provide them. They ended their second day with no more food in their bellies than had been found on the trail. In the Twilight Dells this was not much.

As the fire reached its zenith from the thawed wood, all three of them seemed to have the same thought at the same moment. Greylock saw the old man and Mara looking at him, and when he raised his eyebrow, she answered him.

"Yes, Greylock. Your hair has become more gray!"

That night Greylock had the first of his distressing dreams of Wyrrs calling to him, beseeching him for help. When he awoke in fright, he could not remember the reason for their pleas—yet the prayers directed to him had seemed proper. He shook off the nightmare as nonsense.

Yet the land of the Wyrrs undeniably disturbed him and he could not say why.

The next morning, as they prepared to leave on what the old man had promised could be the last leg of their journey through the Twilight Dells, Greylock sighted a huge column of curling black smoke hovering above the normally white mists of the dells. He was strangely certain that the dark haze was hovering over exactly the same valley from which they had escaped the day before.

Mara looked up quickly from her task of gathering the bedrolls when he pointed out the unusual sight, flicking hair from her eyes. Then she turned to Moag accusingly. "Grandfather! There was no need to punish the Wyrrs. They have suffered enough!"

"It is not my doing!" Moag seemed as puzzled by the smoke as they were. "I did not create a fire; I used a simple smoke spell. It should have been blown away by the winds long ago."

The three of them watched the smoke rise over the Twilight Dells a while longer in silence, each lost in his own thoughts. Greylock was remembering the children, with the huge eyes and bloated stomachs, and wondered if they had escaped the fire. Even the Wyrrs did not deserve to die such a horrible death.

"Perhaps, in the confusion, the fire got away from them," Mara said quietly, but Greylock did not believe it. Something must have happened to the Wyrrs after they had left, he thought. Though he did not say so, for fear of frightening the others, he kept a close watch on the trail behind them as they started on the day's journey.

Just as he feared, the sun had not long risen above the horizon before he caught a glimpse of movement behind him. He watched a little more carefully—but not, he hoped, too noticeably—and this time he was rewarded with the fleeting sight of half a dozen dark figures among the trees. They were still some distance away, but Greylock had no doubt that their own small party had been sighted as well. He did not believe the followers could be Wyrrs, for those strange people could not be seen if they did not wish to be, and they would even now be swarming down upon them.

Greylock had a sudden sick certainty that he knew who was causing the swath of destruction through the Twilight Dells. He was surprised and alarmed that any of his own people would have dared to come this far, but perhaps they had also discovered that the "demons" were not as deadly as they had been taught. The Wyrrs would not be able to stand against the soldiers of the High Plateau during the daylight, he knew, though from what the old man had said, the Wyrrs were formidable on their own land by night.

And yet, Greylock still did not say anything to the others. Instead, he took the lead from the old man, and used his new sense of the land to lead them more quickly through the winding valleys. Moag relinquished the lead without comment, not objecting even when Greylock purposely led them very close to the fortresses of the Wyrrs. But he quickly saw that he could not shake his pursuers this way, or leave them behind. As the trackers gained steadily on the trio, Greylock took the only course he hoped could frustrate the pursuers, a course that appeared equally hazardous to the three partners. If he could just provoke the Wyrrs to come out, he thought, perhaps the followers would be waylaid.

By now even Mara was looking over her shoulder, aware that they were being followed. It was she who let out the shout of surprise that alerted the others to the presence of three men in their path.

Two of the men were dressed like Greylock, though they had evidently not discarded as many layers of clothes—no doubt because they meant to return as soon as possible to their homeland. The soldiers stood on their toes, with their swords ready, should Greylock decide to rush them with the big sword that hung from his belt.

The third man stood idly, casually, between them with a grin of triumph. The man was tall and dark, and wore a single, heavy red robe. Perched on his shoulder was a black crow, the silhouette of which was stitched onto the uniforms of the soldiers.

"Well, Greylock!" the man said. "You did mean what you said, and I see that you were right. There are no such beings as demons—though some of the denizens of this loathesome land come very close!"

"Go back, Redfrock!" Greylock answered in despair. "I was banished by my uncle from the High Plateau, and I have left as I was commanded. You have no authority here!"

"Of course I have authority! I have six soldiers—while you have an old man and a girl. I am

64

surprised that you were able to survive your trek through this horrible land. True, these beings that have pestered us are weak and unskilled opponents; but by their very numbers and persistence, they have taken the lives of fully half my men."

"So you have been burning their houses," Greylock said bitterly. He saw no way of escaping the Steward and his soldiers.

"Are you ready to go back, Prince Greylock? You have proven that there are no demons, but what of the gods? Do you not wish to investigate them as well?"

"I do not know if there are gods or not," Greylock said defiantly. "But I do know that no one can survive the snows of Godshome. You are going to have to remove me from the Three Tiers of Existence altogether, Redfrock!" With this he drew the replica of Thunderer, and the morning light caught the burnished metal in a blinding ray.

The two soldiers gasped and backed away from the sword, but Redfrock quickly recovered. "It is a fake, you fools! Did you not see Thunderer in the hands of the Tyrant?"

The soldiers hesitantly advanced on Greylock, and then moved more boldly as the other four soldiers the Steward had spoken of came from the trees behind them to join in the battle.

Greylock hoped that the wizard had been thinking of some way to use his magic while this talk had been going on; and hoped that Moag remembered that the men of the High Plateau were unaware of magic and would use his power to its most startling effect.

Then two things happened simultaneously to save the three partners. Out of the trees, on all sides of the clearing, came the Wyrrs that Greylock had sensed earlier. And from his two partners came the magic he had hoped could extricate them from the Wyrrs.

As the advancing soldiers stopped and looked at the pitiful army rushing toward them uncertainly, the ground before them exploded in flames. The fire was whipped to a deadly height by a sudden mysterious morning gale, and the partners began to retreat. The wind would not have kept away the soldiers of the High Plateau for long, but the Wyrrs were unable to stand before it and rolled away like the dried stalks of a bush.

The Wyrrs turned their fury on the men of the High Plateau, who sliced through them with their swords as if they were merely practicing the art of war, instead of waging it. But the Wyrrs kept coming, climbing over the bodies of their brothers, and the last sight Greylock had before they left the valley was of the Steward Redfrock, standing in the middle of the little circle of his men, shouting orders while they were being overwhelmed by the vast numbers of Wyrrs. The black crow hovered over the fight, cawing.

Greylock doubted that the entire company of soldiers would be destroyed, yet he was not worried any longer of pursuit, for he did not believe the Steward would try to follow him. If half of Redfrock's company had already been killed in the Twilight Dells, Redfrock would be thinking that he would need an equal number to make it back to the mountains; even then, it would be close. Besides, the Steward would now have the mysterious fire and sudden wind to think about.

But Greylock was not at all content with just escaping alive from the encounter. Steward Redfrock now knew that his opponent was alive—and would undoubtedly be waiting for Greylock if he returned to the High Plateau. A surprise attack would be much harder now, if not impossible.

Mara and her grandfather were breathing hard at the pace he was setting, but he did not slow down until he was well away from the Wyrrs, and the sun was almost gone. They had not yet asked him about the strangers who had attacked them; apparently there was no need to explain who they were.

"Thank you for using your wind-magic, Mara," he said, when he at last slowed the pace. "I know how you hate to use it."

"I did not use my wind-magic!" she said, and Greylock was unable to tell if she spoke the truth. "I do not know where that wind came from."

Moag could not hold back a smile. "It was just a coincidence, Mara?"

"Yes!" Her tone would brook no more questions, and she said nothing more as they set camp for the night.

Again Greylock had a dream of the Wyrrs, and when he awoke in the morning, more of his hair had turned gray.

Chapter Three

Greylock was able to detect that they were leaving the Twilight Dells by the same mysterious sense which had made him notice the sickness of the land. Bad patches of ground still existed, and the terrain looked no different, but already he could feel some changes in the earth. Parts of this land felt fertile and rich.

"Where are we now?" he was finally moved to ask.

Moag seemed a little surprised by the question, and frowned as if he were about to ask how his partner could have known. To Greylock's relief, he did not pose the question. He knew he could ask the old man what it meant to have this feeling of the land, but for some reason he wished to keep it to himself; to reveal it when it was least expected. Besides, he guessed that the wizard suspected some kind of power in his new master, but had not quite admitted to himself that it could be beyond his own knowledge.

"We are leaving the Twilight Dells," Moag said finally—as Greylock had thought he would. "Soon we will be on the borders of Far Valley, and at its center is the BorderKeep. The ruler is an officious man whose army is unfortunately mighty. He once tried to enlist me in his service. He even forced me to wield my fire-magic for him. Me! I would never serve such a fool willingly, you can be sure of that."

"Old man," Greylock said. "I believe you dislike more people than I like."

"Nevertheless, we will avoid the BorderKeep, I think," the wizard said forbiddingly. "The Lord High Mayor may be dangerous, if only because he commands a people far more worthy than he. I do not understand why they have not thrown him out long ago. But people like being dictated to, I always say. We must journey beyond Far Valley, to the first of the fiefdoms of Trold, to get the kind of help we need."

Small and unimportant Far Valley may have been to the worldly-wise wizard, but to Greylock it was a fascinating glimpse of how the people of the Underworld lived; unaware of their luxury, ignorant of poverty.

On the High Plateau, only the Tyrant and his family lived so well. The very lack of food and warmth helped the citizens accept the cruel religion of the Gatekeepers, which said that any person who could no longer produce for the benefit of all—especially for the benefit of the royal family—should seek the "comfort of the gods." All but the most hopeful of the elderly and the sick knew that this meant death, but the sleep on the snows was a better end than some other fates the Tyrant and Steward could subject them to. It was not to the Tyrant's advantage to increase the food supply, or improve the life of his people. As long as the harsh religion of the Gatekeepers kept the people of the High Plateau in his thrall, the Tyrant would never question the priests—even if it meant the exile of his nephew. Greylock was determined to change this state of affairs.

But here, at the border of a huge green valley, stretching as far as the eye could see, even the lowest commoner lived well. Greylock expected to find a contented, even smug people living here, but the old man explained that, even in this seeming paradise, there were grumbles against the Lord High Mayor. Greylock was surprised that the lavish bounty he was seeing seemed to make no difference in their dissatisfaction with life, and mentioned this to Moag.

"Don't be a fool," the wizard said. "If ever you are Tyrant, you must remember to keep your people always scrambling for sustenance. Don't make the mistake of many lesser men, and give them comfort and hope. For if they have food and a warm place to sleep, they will begin to demand something more—such as liberty and power. And these things are much harder for a ruler to give his subjects. Many rulers I have advised, but none could accept this."

"Truly, you have grown cynical in your wanderings, old man," Greylock said lightly. "Does a king rule for himself, or for the benefit of his people? Why else should he be king if he does not mean to help his own kind?"

"You have yet to learn from *your* travels, Prince Greylock," Moag snapped. "You may believe that when you become Tyrant you will improve the lives of your people, and for a short time you may even try that impossible task. If you are lucky, you will fail miserably. Only then, if your people haven't already thrown you out for upsetting things, will you begin the true role of Tyrant—to tell your people what they must do. It will not matter if you are right or wrong, or how much you enrich yourself; they will accept it as long as you rule with an iron fist."

"That would be an irresponsible use of power! I will wield my power to help my people, not harm them! One man—even if he be Tyrant—can never be more important than all his subjects."

"Every man is prey to the temptations of power. Once you have it, Prince Greylock, you will use it. Is not my own subjugation proof of my argument?"

Greylock was struck silent at this. The wizard had touched a sensitive nerve. Why *had* he held the wizard against his will—when it was also against all the principles he had just so glibly proposed? The wizard continued his argument, knowing he had scored a point.

"The ruler who is willing to sacrifice his own welfare for the people is rare; for being the lord of a country makes life all the sweeter, and harder to give up.''

"Do not listen to him," Mara said in disdain. "If he were such a good advisor, then why are we destitute and pledged to a prince without a kingdom? Wizards are no wiser than anyone else, Prince Greylock, though they would like you to think so. Why else do you suppose my grandfather cultivates his every wrinkle? He hopes that an appearance of great age will bring respect. His greatest grudge is that his hair will not turn white. Instead, his back stoops until he is bent over—which of course brings laughter, not respect.''

"Quiet, Granddaughter! I will not take much more of this insolence!" Moag muttered this with sinister overtones, but the girl just hurrumphed and shook her head.

The wizard spoke on confidentially to Greylock, while Mara continued to make scornful noises behind them. "My granddaughter entered my life too late to see the influence I could wield if I wished to. But there are more important things than being rich. I'd rather be poor and free, than serve another. Only by trickery will I serve now!''

As they began descending the short slope to the lush floor of the valley, and over well-tended fields, the girl and the old man began to argue again. This time Greylock let them debate and did not try to soothe tempers. He had learned that the two wrangled endlessly, but without rancor or grudges. Despite her harsh words, Mara's hands would often rest companionably on her grandfather's hunchback.

Instead, Greylock's eyes were drawn to the small town they were approaching. It was set in the middle of the checkerboard fields, and was without defenses. Except for the broad main avenue, it was without perceivable order or planning. Apparently these people had little to fear from their neighbors, Greylock thought, for the town gave more a sense of openness than the militarism that the old man had implied. It was further proof that the Wyrrs were somehow chained and isolated in their poor valleys, when such a rich land lay undisturbed so nearby.

They passed through an orchard of apple trees whose bare limbs were covered by a light green moss, which seemed to glow unnaturally in the afternoon's light. There was green grass, and trees and hedges grew between the thatched roof houses; a natural and appealing landscape that had been so domesticated over the years that the trunks of the trees were worn with familiar touches, and the grass was well-trodden with paths meandering from doorstep to doorstep. All this he saw from a distance, for the wizard would go no closer.

Greylock compared this peaceful scene with his homeland, where even the poorest commoner had to struggle to maintain a secure snowcastle, and where slamming doors were likely to greet the sound of even a friend's approach. There, grudges and vendettas were the overriding concerns of the royal family, and most of the citizens. What must it be like to live in such a peaceful land? Could the wizard be right, and the people have turned their attention to conquest and anarchy? He doubted it, for the town was too quiet and serene to contain such a threat. The military name of BorderKeep was misleading, he thought.

Yet Greylock was soon to learn the meaning of the old wizard's warning. As they tried to detour around this seemingly serene village, a troop of soldiers rushed from the peaceful houses, bristling with armor and weapons.

Greylock stared at them in astonishment, and had to withhold his first impulse to laugh. He didn't know whether to be impressed or to ridicule the costume nature of their uniforms. Bright blue, with silver and gold trimmings, the plump Keepsmen looked sweaty and uncomfortable under the thick layers of brocade. They frowned determinedly at his grin, so Greylock decided it best not to laugh. These men were dressed almost as magnificently as his uncle, adorned in his royal robes! The people of the High Plateau surely did not lack an appreciation of pomp.

Greylock guessed that he could fight his way free, but again he knew he would have to leave the other two behind. He was beginning to wonder if he would not be better off alone. So far, the old man's magic had only saved them from his own miscalculations.

Greylock hesitated at the commands from the soldiers to surrender, but when they tried to take his replica of Thunderer, he rebelled.

He drew the sword with a flourish, and the Keepsmen jumped back in alarm, eyeing the long blade uneasily. Greylock was left standing alone within a circle of a dozen nervous men, turning immediately at the sound of any movement to face the threat. The stalemate looked as though it would not be broken soon, and Greylock hoped that his two companions were mumbling their spells for an escape from this trap.

But Moag and Mara were outside the circle, held immobile by five or six soldiers who were carefully guarding their prisoners, obviously relieved to be out of the fray. The wizard and his granddaughter showed no sign of concocting the magic in their grasp to help in an escape. Greylock realized that he would have to kill several of these ridiculous soldiers, and leave his two partners behind, if he wished to gain his own freedom.

He lowered his blade a little at this thought, and at the same moment most of the soldiers attacked, for they saw that Greylock had no intention of defending himself. Greylock let himself be stripped of Thunderer and dragged before the Lord High Mayor's Palace.

Greylock guessed it was the Lord High Mayor's Palace, because it was the only building in the BorderKeep with the same pretensions of luxury as the uniforms. The other huts were simple and rustic, as befitted a farming people. But this residence was complimented by gables and arches, obviously tacked on over the original structure. The same man who had commissioned the ridiculous uniforms of his guards must have also had this built, Greylock thought. Over the large doors hung a huge Glyden seal of the Lord High Mayor's office, and Greylock noticed that the wizard Moag's eyes immediately filled with yearning.

"Do not tell him anything," the wizard hissed urgently as they were brought toward the grinning Mayor, seated on the top step of his splendid home.

The master of the Palace was surprisingly sedate, however. Taller and leaner than his fellow Keepsmen, the man obviously had an appreciation for style in his own clothing and manner that was not apparent in his subjects and his house. In contrast to the soldiers, he was dressed simply in a green robe and was unarmed.

Perched on the shoulders of the Lord High Mayor, Greylock was dismayed to observe a large white rat. The beady black eyes of the animal stared back at Greylock almost intelligently, until they closed briefly in a satisfied blink. The rat was burrowed comfortably under the long red hair of his master. Greylock shuddered, for on the High Plateau the rat was a competitor for the limited grain, and bounties were set for their bodies. He had never heard of one becoming a pet.

"It is his Familiar," Moag whispered. "If there is one act of magic I would take back if I could, it would be the giving of intelligence to that noisome animal." He sighed. "But there seemed to be no other way of being released, and it seemed a simple price at the time. The rat is much more evil than I had expected. Do not be confused as to who the real ruler of this town is, Prince Greylock."

"You served him?"

"Yes, but only because he trapped me," Moag looked at Greylock with accusing eyes. "Do not make the mistake of believing that these foolish pretensions of the Lord High Mayor are all there is to the man. I call him a fool, but he is much more. He is a very evil man."

"Why do you need fear him, Moag? These

guards of his do not appear very formidable."

"These are just Mayor Tarelton's personal bodyguards and servants, and as I said, only fools would serve him," the wizard said, dismissing their escort. "The citizens of the BorderKeep are the real power here, if they would just wake up and throw off the yoke of the Lord High Mayor. But they do not realize that they are being used for evil."

The Keepspeople were slowly coming out of their houses and trickling in from the fields to watch the unusual parade. One of the farmers especially caught Greylock's attention. The man was sweaty and his clothes were stained from a long day's work in the fields, but he shouldered his way to the front of the crowd without a protest from others, and watched the proceedings intently. What Greylock noticed first was the farmer's size. He was as tall as Greylock, and as dark—darker when the tanned skin was considered—but he was twice as broad as Greylock. Yet the visitor to the BorderKeep could see the intelligence in the man's eyes as he felt himself scrutinized calmly. The old wizard was right in his estimation of the Town's potential, if this was a speciman typical of the men of the BorderKeep. With a sword in that bulky arm, and with training, the man would be an awesome opponent.

"Step forward, my friends," the Lord High Mayor said amiably in a high voice, bringing Greylock's attention back to what was facing him. "I apologize for my overly efficient guards. I understand there was almost a fight! For this you must forgive me. There was no need to greet you with weapons!" He turned his eyes to Greylock, obviously meaning to display most of his charm toward him. "I am Lord High Mayor Tarelton, and this is the BorderKeep."

When the man turned his attention to Moag, he could not hide his dislike. "Welcome back, old man! Have you come back for more Glyden? You did not stay long enough last time to be paid properly. I would be very happy to employ you again, if you wish. Our last association was most profitable, though it ended badly. Still, I am willing to forgive you."

"I would never serve you again, Tarelton!" the magician said bluntly.

The Lord High Mayor winced, and a brief cloud of disappointment crossed his face. At the end of his speech, he also nodded once to Mara—as if he knew that it was through the girl he had his best chance of reaching the wizard. When she turned away stonily, the Lord High Mayor flushed in anger.

Greylock, who was feeling relieved at their welcome shift from prisoners to guests, interjected hastily. "Moag means that he cannot serve you, Lord High Mayor. I have employed him for the time being, for a minor service—which unfortunately will take some time."

"I see!" Mayor Tarelton could not contain his anger. "Who, if I may also be blunt, are you?" The rat seemed to be nuzzling his master's ear, and even from several yards away, Greylock could hear the snuffling sound. Then he realized with some horror that the animal was communicating with the Mayor!

"My name is Greylock," he said finally.

"Where do you come from, Greylock?" A moment of puzzlement showed in the man's otherwise assured voice. "I have never seen you before and I do not think you could be one of the Wyrrs, despite your gray hair. None are so bold, or so healthy as you. If you have come from the east, it would have been reported to me that you had crossed the borders. Therefore, you must have come from the west, and the mountains—the land of the gods." He smiled. "Tell me then, are you a god?"

"I come from the west." Let him think what he will, Greylock thought.

The smile quickly fell from the Lord High Mayor's face. "Perhaps if you do not wish to answer my questions, you would rather stay a night in our prison. At least, until we find that you are not a spy or saboteur! How are we to know if you do not answer our questions?"

"Lord High Mayor Tarelton!" It was the big man whom Greylock had noticed earlier who spoke up to save him. "Why don't you let them be? Do we want the world to think that the Border-Keep is inhospitable to its visitors?"

To Greylock's surprise, the Lord High Mayor addressed the farmer with respect. "Do you now wish to join in my administration of the Border-Keep—as I have offered to you so many times, yeoman Harkkor?"

The big man lowered his eyes and growled, "You know I want nothing to do with it, Tarelton."

Greylock could see the Mayor's relief that he

had not been challenged, nor his proposal accepted. Couldn't anyone else see that? The man's anger seemed to have left him at the interruption. The Lord High Mayor looked down upon the bejeweled sword of Thunderer on his lap, fingering it appreciatively. Then, with obvious reluctance, he extended it hilt first to Greylock.

The man from the High Plateau, who had learned much about the value of Glyden since he had left, now reflected cynically that the Mayor must have decided that there was more Glyden and jewels where the sword had come from. Now all of Tarelton's words and efforts would no doubt be directed toward finding out exactly where that was.

"Yes, well no matter where you are from or who you are, you are welcome to the BorderKeep, Greylock." The Lord High Mayor seemed to have regained his charm—and all his cunning. "My guards will show you to your rooms, where you will find food. Sleep tonight in peace and we can talk on the morrow."

Greylock noticed several things during that first audience with the Lord High Mayor. First of all, the people of the BorderKeep did not appear to like Tarelton. There was more fear than respect in their glances. Secondly, that they had looked at him hopefully when they heard that he had come from the mountains. And last, that the yeomen farmers and wives did not know their own strengths. They could have easily overthrown the Lord High Mayor, and defeated his little army. Greylock could only wonder why they had not already done so.

Throughout the audience, the man the Lord High Mayor had called Harkkor had watched him with intently questioning eyes. Obviously the big man was the leader of the opposition in the BorderKeep, for Greylock had seen that the looks of respect the Mayor had failed to get were directed instead at the big farmer. Harkkor may not know it, Greylock thought, but he already possessed the support he would need to take Tarleton's place. Again, he wondered why this had not already happened.

The answer, he thought, somehow lay in the Familiar. It was the second time he had seen an evil and ambitious man with an unusual pet. Now that he had come to the Underworld, and had seen magic at work, Greylock was becoming certain that the black crow of the Steward was more than a pet.

The three prisoners—or guests, Greylock still wasn't sure which—were taken inside to a large comfortable room, furnished, Greylock guessed from Moag's mumbles, by the old magician's over-luxurious imagination. As the guards in their blue uniforms left them, the wizard muttered at his handiwork.

"I overdid the uniforms, I guess."

"Ghastly," Greylock agreed. "No other army will ever take them seriously again. A suitable revenge, I'd say."

"You think so?" The old man brightened at this idea; but then he continued cursing the Lord High Mayor bitterly.

"I do not understand your hate, Moag," Greylock said at last, for he was enjoying the sudden comfort of the room. "This Mayor Tarelton does not appear to be a very evil man. In fact, I was thinking of asking him for the help we need."

"No! I will not ask that man for help again. I do not trust him. Not for all the Glyden of your kingdom, Prince Greylock!"

"Why not, old man?" Greylock was puzzled by the wizard's vehement rejection. "He has enough soldiers, he is close, and unless I am mistaken, he will be more than willing to help us—for a price. But will not the King of Trold also have a price? As for his faults, I can see that he is greedy. But will we find a better man among the fiefdoms of Trold? As for trusting him, remember he will have to trust me as well, and I know the High Plateau far better than he ever will. He will need me, whereas he will know that I can get the help I need from anywhere."

"I will not serve under him, or with him either!" the wizard said stubbornly. "He is evil, I tell you!" He stomped over to reflect bitterly on the Glyden seal hanging just below the window. He refused to answer Greylock's questions, no matter how much he pleaded with him. Finally, Greylock looked at Mara helplessly, and she explained her grandfather's anger.

"You do not know the customs of wizards, Prince Greylock. In the eastern lands, no ruler would dare force a wizard to serve against his will. There is said to be a mortal curse on such an action. But the Lord High Mayor does not know our customs or does not care, and he dared to betray my grandfather—forcing him to serve on pain of death. And he did not even pay in Glyden!

Moag is bitter that the forces of magic have not destroyed the Lord High Mayor, and have even allowed him to flourish."

"Perhaps such curses take time."

"So I have told him. I have assured him that Mayor Tarelton will someday pay with a horrible fate, but he still doubts the justice of the gods."

"Am I in danger of this curse?"

"He entered your service willingly, Prince Greylock, though he may not stay in your service by his own will." She looked at him sharply. "Do not break your promise to me to free him on the High Plateau, or you will have *my* curse!"

Suddenly, Moag's enraged voice boomed across the room. "Quiet, you fools! That accursed Familiar listens to our every word."

Greylock and Mara looked up to where the mage pointed and saw the rat, half hidden in the folds of a tapestry, watching with coal black eyes. At that moment, the base of a brass candleholder crashed only inches above the fat creature, creating a new small hole in the wall. The startled rat disappeared into the convenient gap.

"Next time I won't miss," Moag said grimly from behind them. Then the old man moaned and sank into one of the overstuffed chairs, burying his face in his hands.

"We are doomed!" he wailed. "It will tell its master everything. Lord High Mayor Tarelton will never let us go now." He looked up with reddened eyes and glared at them. "You utter fools! Your loose tongues have condemned us. How could you have been so stupid? Did you not realize that everything we say in the Lord High Mayor's

Palace will be overheard?''

Greylock did not have any pity for the old man's troubles this time. Moag's singleminded goal of finding Glyden was beginning to annoy him. If he wanted Glyden so much, why would he not work for it? By honest labor, if he refused to use his magic! Why would he not cooperate and compromise, like anyone else? No wonder the wizard had searched so long without results!

Moag continued his string of recriminations, and Greylock felt himself becoming angry at the name-calling. Finally he marched over to the wizard's chair and loomed over the old man, meaning to teach him a lesson. His shadow fell over the suddenly frightened and wizened wizard, who ceased to speak and melted back into the cushions as far as his huge back would allow him to go. Greylock grabbed him by his shoulders and lifted him bodily from the chair.

''You forget your place, Moag! I am the master and you are the servant. We are not partners any longer, and you had best learn that! I am a prince, and therefore meant by the gods to rule. You are a wizard, and therefore meant to serve. Do not ever call me 'fool' or any other name again!''

Then Greylock's anger had passed as quickly as it had come, and he let go of the old man and looked about him once more in a startled way. Mara was staring at him with shocked eyes. The old wizard was surprisingly frightened and subdued by the berating. Greylock realized that he had let his anger turn to rage, even as he was talking—just as he had so often seen his uncle do—and for which his uncle had always expressed sorrow later. Greylock had not known that he possessed such a temper, perhaps because he had never been frustrated and thwarted before, nor talked to in such a way.

"Greylock!" Mara said finally. "It is only Moag's way! He does not mean anything by it. I doubt he even knows he is rude!"

"Forgive me, Moag," Greylock said, almost sheepishly. "My uncle sent me away to die under the spell of just such an anger. And thus did I provoke him."

"Do not apologize to me!" the wizard said bitterly. "I am only a servant!"

Despite all of Greylock's apologies, the easy camaraderie that had marked their partnership before disappeared, to be replaced by a stiff and formal master-and-servant relationship. From that moment onward, Greylock could see the resentment in the wizard grow. Trying to make amends, he said, "If it will make you feel safe, I will not have anything to do with the Lord High Mayor."

But the old man was not mollified.

That night Greylock had his most vivid dream of the Wyrrs, though he had hoped that once out of the Twilight Dells they would go away. It seemed to him that the Wyrrs were right there, in Border-Keep, scratching at the second-story windows of the Palace and looking at him with wide, pleading eyes. He woke from the eerie dream breathing heavily and sweating, and it took him several minutes to realize that there was indeed a sound at the window; a sort of *ping,* as if the window were assailed by a hailstorm. Getting from the soft bed, he drew on his clothes and picked up Thunderer before he made his way to the window.

Not knowing what to expect, he stared down on the moonlit town square. Finally he saw the shadow of a huge man standing under a tree, waving for him to come down. From the size and shape of the man, Greylock recognized yeoman Harkkor.

The Palace, for all its ostentatious show, afforded Greylock with few places for his feet, but it proved no real obstacle to his climbing skill, even without his Talons. He could see the admiring look in the yeoman's eyes as he dropped silently the last few feet to the ground. But the farmer hushed him when he gave a whispered greeting, and led Greylock away from the building's walls.

"The Mayor is going to offer you the use of his army, in return for what he believes to be your vast riches," the yeoman whispered. "After that, he no doubt will try to betray you, but I do not know this for a fact. My people—the common folk of BorderKeep—would like for you to accept his offer. We know that it is a great deal to ask, to bring such a viper into your land, but we ask it of you nonetheless."

"But why?"

"Little can be done against the Lord High Mayor while he is still within the BorderKeep." Greylock could hear contempt in the man's tone. "His spies are everywhere. If they cannot gain entrance, his rat Familiar will find a way. No discussion can occur in the BorderKeep between more than a few honest men without his hearing of it, and every word that was said being reported. It is our hope that away from BorderKeep—with, or

86

without your help, for we have no right to ask you—Tarelton can at last be overthrown."

"Will you be joining our expedition, yeoman Harkkor?"

The big man smiled. "Yes, though it may raise suspicions, for I have never joined the Lord High Mayor in his conquests, I have decided to come along this time."

"Then I will do as you ask. I would not trust the Lord High Mayor without someone like you in his army to turn to if need be. But I am not sure that it is necessary for you to go to such lengths. Mayor Tarelton is afraid of you already. He knows that the people of BorderKeep would follow you if you asked them."

"Perhaps, but I must be sure for their sake. Now, I must go. The longer we tarry here, the more chance of us being discovered. Tell no one of our conversation. Be assured that you will have allies within the Lord High Mayor's army." The farmer began to move away.

"Wait!" Greylock knew his voice had almost become audible to those within the Palace, and he dropped his voice. "I must tell Moag!" he hissed. "I told the old man I would never join the Mayor. He already believes that I have betrayed him once, and I could not do this without saying why."

"No!" Yeoman Harkkor was adamant. "The wizard's hate is too noticeable. It must remain in his eyes, or the Lord High Mayor will know something is wrong."

Reluctantly, Greylock let the man go, and climbed silently back up the Palace walls. He had no more dreams of the Wyrrs, but his sleep was not peaceful.

The next morning, as yeoman Harkkor had predicted, the guards came to fetch Greylock for an audience with the Lord High Mayor. The gloomy wizard and Mara were to be left behind, with the not-very-believable explanation that the Lord High Mayor wished to talk privately with his old friends later.

"Don't go, Greylock," Moag pleaded, his hate of the Mayor coming through again.

"He already knows everything, Moag. I may as well hear what he has to say." Greylock fingered the hilt of Thunderer, reassured by its feel, and even more so by the ludicrous appearance of the soldiers of the Palace.

"Don't listen to him, Greylock!" Moag called out after him as he followed the guards from the room. "You will regret it!"

Apparently, Moag had not had a chance to work his magic on the dining room. The two servants, dressed in a garish red, were the only glaring luxuries in a room made up entirely of wood. Greylock guessed that, despite the splendor of the Lord High Mayor's Palace and the rich uniforms of his soldiers, the Mayor was in reality quite poor, and that the wizard Moag had been the only good thing to happen to him for some time. Only the seal of Glyden above the doors of the Palace showed that there might be a wealth of metal and gems in the BorderKeep, and Greylock suspected that the Mayor had stripped his people to come up with a melting of that much of the precious metal.

Greylock had already dismissed most of the wizard's objections to the Lord High Mayor, and he intended to enlist him as an ally as the yeoman had asked. Still, he waited for the other man to make the proposal, as he was sure he would. The greed that had shown in the Mayor's face each time Greylock allowed him a view of the hilt of Thunderer was laughably obvious.

"Come in, Prince Greylock," the Lord High Mayor welcomed him—by a title he should not have even known. "We serve ourselves, mostly. Let us eat before we talk. I know the wizard Moag could not supply food for your long journey, so you are no doubt still hungry."

Greylock was ravenous, for he had chosen to rest rather than eat the night before. The servants stood back from a table laden with a bounteous measure of simple but filling food, and watched with amused eyes as Greylock eagerly began heaping the food onto a plate. The last bowl was full of leafy lettuce, and as he started to scoop it up, he saw something moving in the greenery. Jumping back with an astonished shout, he barely avoided upsetting his plate, and that of the Lord High Mayor's. The head of the Familiar, seemingly puzzled by Greylock's reaction, emerged to peer over the lip of the bowl.

"I am disappointed in you, Prince Greylock." Mayor Tarelton appeared more amused than disappointed, his guest saw. "My rat is really quite tame and harmless, and very useful." The hint about the rat's usefulness made Greylock conscious that the other man was leading up to his proposal.

"In the land I come from, rats are neither tame nor harmless, and certainly not useful."

"Is it true you come from the west? From the mountains?"

Greylock looked at the rat significantly. It was now eating contentedly from the plate of his master. Greylock had suddenly lost his appetite and picked at the food in a desultory fashion, wondering if the rat always had the run of the table.

The Lord High Mayor answered the look with a smile. "Yes, if what you were telling the magician was the truth, then I also know the truth. I know that you had intended to ask me for help, if it hadn't been for that interfering old wizard. By the way, I would advise you to get from Moag what you can, and then let him go as soon as possible. That is what I did. I happen to know that you and he are not friendly. Frankly, I am not surprised, he is a very ungrateful man."

"We had not yet decided to ask you."

"Nevertheless, I accept your proposal. No! I insist. You must allow me to provide you with the military assistance you need to conquer your High Plateau."

So there it was, Greylock thought. Just as the old man had said—they had no choice. Yet Greylock was not dissatisfied with the offer. He was not willing to make another long journey just to quell the old man's fears, even if they could somehow manage to escape. He was tired of the heat and the humidity of the Underworld, and wanted to return to his homeland before every hair on his head had turned gray. He had learned little of Gateway in the Underworld—he would have to return to the High Plateau to find the answer. And finally, Greylock felt a sympathy for the cause of the conspiritors.

Still, the venture was not even to be considered, unless he was allowed to lead it. For this he must remain alive and free. The treacherous Lord High Mayor must be made aware of this.

"We can only succeed if the Steward is removed from our path—and I intend to kill him," he said. "I do not want to harm my uncle. When I show him how wrong he was about the Underworld, he will have to take me back."

"Why must we convince the Tyrant, if we must conquer the High Plateau anyway? He will have to proclaim you his successor."

"There is nothing to be gained by merely conquering the High Plateau," Greylock answered. "The people must be able to accept their sovereign, and they would never accept an Underworlder. So you need me, Lord High Mayor; not just to help you find and conquer my land, but afterwards as well. You will be well paid for your help—in Glyden."

"But of course! It is the Glyden I want, as you have already so astutely pointed out to Moag. There is one other matter, though, that I feel I must bring up with you. Must you have the wizard and his granddaughter along? The old man seems to have a grudge against me, and might do something hasty. That would ruin all of our plans. We do not need him, for my army is sufficient, I assure you."

"Moag is in my service. Why do you object to him?"

"He believes that I forced him to serve me, but I never once threatened him. It is all in his mind. He

91

has an irrational hate of me, as you have seen."

Perhaps the Mayor had not threatened Moag, Greylock thought—perhaps not in so many words. But he had already seen how the Lord High Mayor could hint with vague and sinister overtones.

Apparently, Mayor Tarelton did not believe that he could restrain the magician from casting his spells. It might prove useful in keeping his new ally in line later, Greylock thought, if he continued to believe this. There was no sense in telling him that no prince of the High Plateau would abandon a friend.

"Moag may be very useful in this adventure," he said simply. "Be assured that I will try my best to keep him from using his powers in any way that could be harmful to you."

Lord High Mayor Tarelton did not seem comforted by this statement, but they shook hands over the arrangement. Both of them inwardly vowed not to trust the other. The Mayor may have his Familiar, Greylock thought, but I have the wizard.

● ● ●

But the Lord High Mayor possessed more than just his own Familiar as a source of information. That night, the Steward Redfrock's crow made three trips over the same terrain it had taken Greylock three full days, and many adventures, to cover. As soon as Tarelton had returned to his own room after dinner, the gist of the conversation was relayed from the Lord High Mayor to his own Familiar, and then from the rat to the Steward's

Familiar. In this way, the crow learned that the Mayor had followed Redfrock's instructions exactly, and it set off toward Godshome.

It flew high over the Twilight Dells, for the land of the Wyrrs disturbed it as much as it had disturbed Greylock, proving perhaps that the Wyrrs were neither good or evil, but had their own secrets. When it had reached the High Plateau, it circled the snowy plain twice in confusion, for it could not sense the presence of its master anywhere on the surface. At last it gave in to the inevitable, and landed near the entrance of one of the many caves that riddled the lava beneath the snows, and which served as convenient passageways for the people of the High Plateau to travel from snowcastle to snowcastle.

To the men working on the new and unnatural passageway that the Steward had ordered built, it was disconcerting to see the big black bird hopping down a passage so far below the earth and away from its natural habitat. Yet, with its coal black eyes, and inky feathers, it appeared horribly at home in the dark.

"Ah, there you are!" the Steward greeted his Familiar as it scratched around the last turn in the new cave, finding its master overseeing the finishing touches of his handiwork. It flew to the Steward's shoulder, the tips of its wings actually brushing the narrow sides of the passage.

"Greylock means to bring an army, does he?" the Steward said when it had reported. "Tell the Lord High Mayor that he has done well, and that he has only one thing he must remember. Tell him that when the time comes for a choice, Prince

Greylock must chose the left-hand course. That is all he must do. Convince Greylock to take the left passage.''

The Familiar jumped from his master's shoulder almost delicately. Then with awesome dignity it left the subterranean caverns for the night skies, and arrived at the Lord High Mayor's Palace just as dawn was breaking. The bemused Tarelton received his instructions while Greylock slept, little suspecting that the long arm of the Steward Redfrock had already touched him in BorderKeep.

Chapter Four

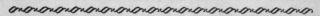

Greylock watched from the first of the foothills, its top sprinkled with the first snows of winter, as the army of the Underworld set off for Godshome a few weeks later. From the hilltop, the soldiers appeared as a line of white shapes, glinting off the rays of the morning sun. He had insisted that the bright colored uniforms be discarded.

"My homeland is a land of snow," he argued. "We do not wish to be targets any more than we have to. Our only chance of success is to surprise the Steward. If your guards approach in those uniforms, we will be seen from miles away!"

When yeoman Harkkor had agreed with Greylock, the Lord High Mayor had no choice but to reluctantly comply, though in protest he had refused to give up his own bright green robe. By now the magnificent uniforms had been replaced by a hastily assembled hodgepodge of white clothing. The Lord High Mayor with his red hair and brilliant robe stood out in this company—as perhaps he wished.

Greylock was beginning to have other doubts as well. It was obvious that the men of Far Valley ate well, but except for the yeomen, without working very hard to take off their fatty weight. Many in the army were huffing and panting long before the first slopes of the mountains had been reached. Their weapons now seemed in many cases more ornamental than deadly, their determined faces only ludicrous. Greylock was irritable this morning, for he had had another frightening—and inexplicable—dream of Wyrrs calling to him, the night before.

Luckily, yeoman Harkkor had persuaded many of his fellow farmers to come along, and this sturdy component of the army, with their wickedly sharp scythes, reassured Greylock that his expedition was not a foolish venture. When the Lord High Mayor had found it impossible to talk the yeomen out of joining his army, as was their right, he had begun to defer to Yeoman Harkkor, apparently hoping in this way to placate the farmers.

Moag had come along as well, grumbling—though never to Greylock's face. He had begged Greylock to reconsider the alliance with the Lord High Mayor, insisting that he could whisk them away with the help of his magic.

"You will regret this, Prince Greylock!" he warned again. "You have made a compact with a demon!"

"Oh, come now, Moag." The temptation to tell the old man about his talk with Harkkor was strong, but he remembered the farmer's warning about spies. "You can always whisk us away later. Mayor Tarelton is just a very greedy man."

"He is more than just greedy! There *are* 'demons,' you know," the wizard said cryptically. "Just because you have not found them yet does not mean they do not exist. Evil spirits are all about, and I summoned one by mistake when I created that Familiar."

Mara had fallen silent since Greylock's outburst of three weeks before, and he wondered if he had frightened her with his temper. So it was that he found himself marching alone, at the head of the long column.

They soon entered the Twilight Dells, and Greylock reflected on the accuracy of the name. Though it was only a little past noon as they entered the first narrow glen, and though the sky was cloudless, a pall seemed to have descended over the light and the company. Greylock felt the same revulsion to the land that he had experienced before.

Though none of the people known as Wyrrs revealed themselves to the armed body of soldiers, the Keepsmen looked about them nervously. Apparently, Moag had not bothered to ask the men of the BorderKeep the reason why the Twilight Dells were out of bounds. It seemed evident they knew the secret. Greylock approached the

Lord High Mayor, concealing a shudder at the sight of the ever-present rat Familiar.

"Why are your people afraid, Mayor Tarelton?"

"It is superstition," the Lord High Mayor said with a great display of scorn; but it was apparent from his darting eyes that he too was frightened. "No matter how educated my people become, they still cling to their fears. Legends of this poor land tell of a deed so dreadful that the Wyrrs are forever haunted by it, and the land cursed."

"What was this great evil?" Greylock asked. He was a little encouraged by the Lord High Mayor's bold posturing. Sometimes such a show could even take the place of courage, which he doubted the Mayor had much of, but would need.

"No one knows. It is long forgotten, or perhaps it was so terrible that the Wyrrs will keep it to themselves until the time of their extinction as a race. The story I heard as a baby on my nurse's lap was that the Wyrrs had betrayed the gods of Godshome, and are condemned to stay in the Twilight Dells until the gods call on them once more for help. But you should know more of this than I, shouldn't you?"

Greylock had no answer. The story sounded very much like the catastrophic closure of Gateway, and the casting-down of the demons. Again there was the uncanny resemblance to the teachings of the Gatekeepers—but distorted, and made more human. He had not thought of the Wyrrs since he had first passed through their valleys, except in his dreams. Now, however, their plight came back to him with such a force that he knew he would never forget them again. He did not know why he should be concerned with the Wyrrs, but their situation was something that he knew would never leave him in peace. Somehow he would have to discover the answer to the Wyrr's curse.

Greylock was not too concerned about an attack, for from what he had seen of the inhabitants of the dells he doubted that they would confront such a large body of armed men. He was surprised therefore to glimpse a host of men filling all of the next valley. Yet these were not the pale, weak humans whom he had seen before, but tall and strong men and women, with dark hair and strong faces. In fact, he thought suddenly, they looked like citizens of the High Plateau!

As the company halted hesitantly at the narrow opening of the valley, many of the Keepsmen looked at him, comparing his tall, dark frame with what they were seeing. Greylock, with his gray hair, was the flawed one compared to these handsome people. But he did not notice these glances, for he was intent on the manner and dress of the strangers. For a few seconds he was certain that he was seeing his own brethren, men of the High Plateau. He began to walk forward eagerly to greet them. Smiles grew on the faces of the strangers at the sight of him.

"Stop!" Moag's voice tugged at Greylock, but the spell was too strong for him and he quickened his step. Suddenly, the old man's hunched, stooped body moved into view with unusual speed, blocking his progress toward the strange assemblage. "Do not go further, Prince Greylock!"

The wizard led Greylock back, dazed and resisting, to the clustered group of Keepsmen, and drew a line in the dust before him. Greylock began to step over it, paying little notice to the action, and drawn once more by the spell of the strangers. His foot would not descend on the far side of the line in the dirt, no matter how much force he used to press it down.

Suddenly, the vision of the others seemed to waver, and the strong, beautiful faces turned into the gaunt white skulls of the Wyrrs. Greylock turned his face from the sight in dismay.

Moag had continued drawing his line and muttering, until he had gone twice around the company of men, gathered at his urging into a tight mass. One by one, the others gasped in dismay as the sight before their eyes changed drastically. When the Wyrrs saw the looks turn to disgust, their own smiles—now grotesque parodies— dropped completely, and the eerie gathering rushed toward the smaller body of men murderously.

At the line in the dust they too were repelled, while the old man muttered furiously under his breath to maintain the spell. The Wyrrs stood only a few terrifying steps away, unable to reach their victims and roaring with a deafening frustration. The afternoon wore on, and the wizard collapsed to the ground muttering his spell with determination that blocked out everything else.

Finally, as night began to fall slowly, the thousands of Wyrrs seemed to lose interest in their siege around the awkwardly gathered company, and began drifting away in small groups. The roar of their cries slowly died down. At last, they were gone and the only sign of their presence was the trampled earth of the empty valley.

Mara and Greylock helped the old wizard up, and for a few moments he was dazed. "I could not have held them back much longer," he sighed finally in relief. "My earth-magic is not strong, and the Wyrrs are at their most powerful by night."

"There were thousands of them!" Greylock said in shock. "I thought you said they hated each other, Moag, and would murder each other outside their own little clans, their own valleys."

"We must have stumbled on one of their ceremonies," the wizard answered solemnly. "It is only when they are gathered together in such numbers that they can summon the power to call back their old appearances. I suspect they cannot often stand this reminder of their past, and it is for this reason they avoid each other."

"What has happened to them?" Greylock was beginning to understand more than he wanted. "Can we not help them?" Despite his own vows of disbelief, the Wyrrs were coming uncomfortably close to the ancient legends of an Underworld of pain and punishment. They were his people, he knew now. The ancestors of the Wyrrs were his ancestors as well.

"You do not wish to know what they did. Help? There is no help for them, though they have their own foolish belief that one day a god will descend from Godshome and lift their curse."

Greylock looked at the wizard curiously. He had been wrong apparently to believe that the old man was unaware of the secrets of the valley. How much else did Moag know and not reveal? There would come a time when he would pry that knowledge from the wizard, he vowed.

The invading army continued toward the Three Peaks of Godshome in the morning, this time not bothering to journey by the circular route of the peaceful valleys, but in a straight line, daring the Wyrrs to try to stop them. Now the Keepsmen were confident and boisterous, but Greylock was still bothered by the confrontation. The army's revelries seemed somehow profane to him, though he should have been encouraged by them. He wondered if they would be so brave if Moag had not already shown that he could repell the Wyrrs with his magic. He noticed the yeoman Harkkor and his followers also seemed to be saddened by the encounter.

Something continued to nag at his memory, something that the Gatekeepers had taught him in his youth—of demons' curses and a prophecy of their Deliverance. Greylock had made his choice not to believe early, though he had once dreamed he could catch that lost word which, could a man but find it, would make him the master of his fate. But he had abandoned the teachings of the Gatekeepers, and thus had never read the sacred books very carefully.

He did not expect to see the ghosts of the Twilight Dells again, but tried to forget them and concentrate on his coming triumph over his uncle. As camp was set for the night, he wandered away from the others and began climbing one of the knolls, to try to restore his confidence.

The spell of the Wyrrs once again fell over him,

and he recognized the landscape of his dreams, though he knew he was awake. The ground before him grew even darker, and his view of the white peaks of Godshome from the knoll was hindered by a blurry vision. He marched toward them, somehow sensing that, though the path was becoming unnatural, it was not he who was in danger. Behind, he could feel the presence of others following him, but it was as if they were not there, and he paid no attention to their worried shouts. The dark trail seemed to slant upward under his feet, though only seconds before it had stretched before him, flat and well lit by the light of a full moon.

He was not surprised this time when out of this dark, the figure of a man emerged, followed by an old woman. The man, who could have been Greylock's twin or perhaps a younger brother, had well-structured dark features. But even under the spell of the Wyrrs, the old woman appeared ancient and ravaged. Greylock was mildly surprised to find a woman that old among the people of the Twilight Dells.

The man raised his hand in greeting, and Greylock stopped and also signed a greeting. The man—or apparition—seemed to be trying to say something to him, but Greylock, as in his dreams, could understand nothing but the urgent need of the stranger. Everything sounded much harsher, yet somehow removed—like someone scratching the glass on the far side of a windowpane.

"He says that the people of the valleys welcome the Deliverer," Mara suddenly said from beside him, and he noticed her presence for the first time, as if she had just stepped into the light. Whatever the meaning of this meeting, it was apparent to Greylock that in some way Mara was to play a role.

"He begs forgiveness for their attacks, but they did not recognize you when you passed before," she translated. "He begs to know when you will return to lead them to their freedom."

Greylock shook his head in puzzlement. "I am not returning! I have nothing to do with his people. I am not this Deliverer he speaks of with such reverence."

Now the old woman stepped forward and started to speak. Her voice was no more than a croak, but Greylock could understand the horrible words without translation.

"You must help the Wyrrs, my son, for your father was one of them. The greatest of their kind since they were so long ago imprisoned. For him I was banished from the High Plateau. Now you must help them."

Greylock was shocked, disbelieving—but he found himself answering. "I will return to help you, when I can. Soon!"

The ghostly figures seemed satisfied with this answer, and disappeared back into the murk. Then suddenly the bright moonlight was back again, and the Lord High Mayor was there, pestering him with questions. Mara and the old wizard were there as well, staring at him with concerned faces. Two of Tarelton's guards had followed, and had drawn their weapons.

"We followed you out here, and found you with the two Wyrrs. What were they saying to you?"

"Wyrrs?" The vision still seemed unreal to

Greylock, and he still was haunted by the image of the woman calling him son.

"You stood there staring at them, Greylock, for several minutes," the Lord High Mayor said in confusion. "Then the old woman spoke to you in a language I did not understand. I could barely keep my men from murdering the Wyrrs in their fear."

Greylock looked about him in a daze. It was apparent from their looks that only the old wizard, and his granddaughter, had seen what he had seen. Only the two with magic running through their veins, he thought, had seen the noble figure of the valley man and a dignified old woman, and not the pathetic visages of Wyrrs. What did it mean?

Only a short while before, he had been interested only in conquering his own homeland, and regaining his right to the throne. He had been in the easy company of the greedy Mayor and the covetous wizard. Now, whether he liked it or not, he was bound to seek the counsel of the Gate-keepers, the teachers against whom he had rebelled and who long ago had given up on their royal student. Perhaps the price would be too high, but Greylock knew he would have to pay it.

There was one other consequence of his meeting with the Wyrrs. As they strolled back into the light of the campfires, he heard Mara gasp.

"Greylock! Your hair has turned completely gray!"

He stared at her in shock, until the wizard summoned a burnished steel shield. "It is true, Prince Greylock. Look for yourself."

The stranger in the mirror of the shield looked like an old man, with young and stunned black eyes. The change was complete.

● ● ●

The next morning found Greylock still feeling the effects of his mysterious meeting of the day before, but he decided he must conceal this from Mayor Tarelton and appear to be concerned only with gaining his rightful throne again. Once more visions of the Lady Silverfrost, and of himself sitting upon the throne of the Tyrant, filled his head. The Lord High Mayor divined the direction of Greylock's thoughts and was reassured.

For a little while, Mayor Tarelton thought, the prince had talked of sacrifices and doing his duty. Now he was back to talking about Glyden, a much safer and more alluring subject. The Mayor was relieved, for the Steward Redfrock's instructions had been clear—to lead Prince Greylock into the trap that was being prepared for him.

It was the cold air of the foothills and sight of snow on the higher elevations that helped restore Greylock's confidence—and the increasing distance from the Twilight Dells. While the others bundled up in extra clothing, Greylock shed some of his, admonishing himself for having fallen into the soft ways of the Underworlders. In spite of this confidence, he concealed the jeweled replica of Thunderer in an ordinary sheath. There would be a proper time to reveal it, he thought.

With his long, eager strides up the twisting mountain trail, he soon grew impatient with the out-of-shape soldiers of the BorderKeep. He wished he could just continue with yeoman

106

Harkkor and his followers, but the farmers had scrupulously avoided calling attention to themselves, and would only acknowledge their agreement with subtle signs. He was also becoming concerned that he had seen no indication of the Steward's sentries. Greylock had expected the Gateway to be rigidly guarded and was beginning to wonder if they were not marching into a trap.

"We must hurry!" he said at last. "If my people choose a successor to my uncle before I return, then we will have to fight a long and bloody war."

"I'm sorry, Prince Greylock," the Lord High Mayor said. "My men are not used to these heights. You must give them a chance to rest."

Moag snorted. "I told you we should have gone on to Trold. King Kasid would have given us a real army, not this fat and lazy bunch of villagers."

"You are a nuisance with all your grumbling, old man," Tarelton retorted angrily.

"Perhaps it will not matter," Greylock quickly intervened. "I must reconnoiter the High Plateau anyway. If we are very lucky, my uncle will still be alive and the succession will not yet have been decided. Rest your men here, Lord High Mayor and proceed—cautiously—in the morning. I will meet you on the trail."

"What if you don't come back?"

"Then I would suggest you turn back, Mayor Tarelton." Greylock smiled grimly. "Our only chance of success is to surprise them. They will never expect anyone to come from the Underworld. They will be fighting among themselves as usual. But if I am captured, there will be no victory for you: if I am dead, they will never accept you as a ruler." Greylock hoped that what he had just said was true, and that the Steward Redfrock had given up watching for him.

"Maybe you had better not go, Prince Greylock," Mayor Tarelton looked worried, and Greylock thought that at least he was taking his ally seriously. He did not realize that the Mayor's instructions were to guide the prince, and that could not be done if he were out of sight.

"Someone must scout ahead, and only I know the way," Greylock said impatiently. "Don't worry! I'll be back in the morning. Come along, Moag. Let us see if anything has changed in my absence. You can finally get a look at our Glyden."

He turned to move up the trail when he heard Mara's soft voice object. "I am coming, too."

"You stay," Greylock answered, more annoyed that she would refute his orders than for any real objections to her coming along.

"You are not my master, Greylock," she said angrily. "I go where Grandfather goes. It has always been so."

"Hold her here for at least an hour," he told yeoman Harkkor, who complied by lifting her with one arm, still struggling, and waving them on their way with the other.

Looking back, Greylock was satisfied to see that his army blended in with the mountain snows, except for the green robe and red hair of the Lord High Mayor, which stood out clearly. He would have to convince the Mayor to give up at least the green robe, he thought, if not his red hair. The two of them quickly left the others behind.

Even so, as they rounded the first turn in the trail, hundreds of yards away, they found Mara standing before them frowning determinedly with her arms crossed.

"How . . . ?" Greylock managed to sputter. "Where did you come from?"

"Well, well!" Moag chuckled, and Greylock turned in astonishment at the happy sound. "Prince Greylock, you have succeeded in making her do what I have been pleading with her, and cajoling her, to do for years. She has used her magic! And without the orders from a master! Her motivation must have been very strong indeed for her to do that. And I do not think it is because she wants to be with her grandfather," he finished, looking at Greylock in appreciation.

Greylock was bewildered further to see a red flush rise in Mara's cheeks. He remembered his earlier promise to himself to look for the truth in her face. But he did not like the truth he was seeing in her face right now. She couldn't be in love with him! She was still a child! And he was promised to the Lady Silverfrost.

But even as he raised his objection to himself, he saw that in their few weeks together she had swiftly grown out of that awkward phase he had first noticed. She was almost a woman! Her bright green eyes suddenly showed a maturity that had not been there before. Her long blond hair no longer had the downy softness of childhood, but the healthy glow of a woman. And her habit of flicking the hair from her eyes was no longer annoying, but alluring. Her slim figure had filled out in a few short weeks. Not knowing what to say in the embarrassed silence, he turned abruptly and brushed by her without further word.

As they ascended into the cloud layer, the two Underworlders grew short of breath and slowed down. Greylock was forced to adjust his long, eager steps to their timid ones. Finally, even he was forced to don his last, heavy robe as the snowflakes began to obscure everything but the next few steps. Greylock found the staff he had cached on the way down, leaving it in the remote hope that he would be able to return. He wished he could have saved his Talons as well. Now the staff proved useful in probing the snow-covered trail. Several times the snowpack fell away into space at the staff's touch, and the three stared down into a sky of whirling snowflakes. Greylock helped the two frightened Underworlders around these spaces as best he could.

Finally, Greylock motioned for them to remain silent and motionless, and inched forward to study something only he could see. He brushed away some of the light powder snow, and then smiled to himself and motioned the others forward.

"We must hurry from here if we are to see anything of the High Plateau before dark."

"How are we to see anything in this blizzard?" Moag said miserably. "I can't even see the trail anymore!"

Both Underworlders were dismayed by Greylock's sudden spurt of speed from this point onward, fearing to see him fall away into the air, but they grew silent when they saw a broad, even road stretching upward before them.

Greylock smiled proudly. "This is the Gateway.

From here on, every road in my uncle's kingdom is paved in stone. And some, as I have told you, in Glyden." I may as well keep up the deception of a Glyden-rich kingdom a while longer, he thought. Even Moag would have to be satisfied when he saw the treasury of the Tyrant.

But for once the wizard was not thinking of Glyden. Instead, he was stooped over even more than usual, examining their broad and magnificent roadway.

"Did your people build this?" he asked wonderingly. "This is a feat of engineering beyond any but the richest of the Kings of Trold!"

"These roads have been here for as long as anyone can remember," Greylock explained. "We have a story that we are simply the Gatekeepers of this road, which we call Gateway in our legends. We are the protectors of Godshome. This has never made much sense to me, for what is there to protect? Could an entire country, an entire people, be only Gatekeepers for others, whom we have never seen? Where are the gods we are meant to protect? Or the demons we are supposed to protect them from? Before I went down into your Underworld, I did not believe any of these stories. Now . . . I am not so sure. It seems to me that there must be a reason for these legends, a reason not even the Gatekeepers, our priests, know."

When they crossed the first bare patches of the road, where the mountain winds had never allowed the snows to build, the deception of a road paved in Glyden was shown up. Instead, the road was made of huge stones, placed in a mosaic that left no gap larger than the sharp edge of a sword.

111

The stones had not been carved, but by an almost unimaginable patience had been laid naturally side by side until they had fitted snugly. Moag was fascinated by the ancient road, and did not complain about the lack of Glyden, if indeed he noticed it.

At one point both Underworlders stopped and let out startled shouts. They had suddenly walked over a patch of the Gateway which radiated a surprising but welcome heat.

"What is the source of this warmth?" Moag asked in amazement.

"It comes out of the mountain," Greylock explained quickly. The two Underworlders were lingering in the comforting heat, despite his urgings to hurry. "Sometimes it comes out of cracks in the earth, sometimes out of the earth itself. Many parts of the High Plateau are fertile enough to grow food because of this warmth, and it is around these warm spots, which we call Icemelts, that we build our snowcastles."

"But what causes the heat?" Moag insisted. As a magician he was not satisfied with this answer, and as a Fire-Wizard he was fascinated by the fire in the earth.

"We do not know where it comes from. Only that it comes from deep within Godshome. Sometimes the very earth is melted and boils out of the cracks in the mountain." A cloud passed over Greylock's face. "When that happens there is much destruction. Many times we have had to rebuild. The Gatekeepers tell us that the whole of the High Plateau was created from this firestone. But they also say that the evil spirits—demons —brew the firestone, so I never believed them. Now . . . I am not so sure.''

It was the second time, he realized, that he had admitted to himself that he might be reverting to the religion of his youth—to the time when he had been fascinated by the Gatekeepers' arcane answers to the mysterious origins of firestone.

Moag and Mara were finally willing to move on, though they continued to linger at each warm spot they came upon. Greylock warned them that staying in the heat only made the inevitable cold worse, but they were unable to resist the seductive pull of the warmth. Greylock began to wonder if he would not have the same trouble with the whole army of Underworlders when he led them this way.

The road began to widen and the slope to level, and Greylock once again moved forward cautiously. At last they sighted the first of the dwellings Greylock had called snowcastles, perched on the very edge of the High Plateau. The plateau dropped off sheerly on the side that was exposed to the sky. The other sides were bound upon by the Three Peaks of Godshome.

But the two Underworlders could not see the peaks in the mild blizzard, and their eyes were drawn to the dwelling, which indeed resembled a huge castle made out of snow. The walls were thick and imposing, towering over the path and out into the empty spaces of the mountain cliffs. Narrow windows had been carved into the sides of the walls, and a tower had been built at one corner. The ice of the tower gleamed blue even in the dim light of the storm. Barely visible within were stone buildings, the true living quarters of the inhabitants. The snowcastle seemed designed to afford a view on all, and access to none.

Greylock pointed proudly. "There lies Castle-Guardian, home of my friend, Mordref, whom I call Slimspear. Only he and my sister, Ardra, know how I left the High Plateau—that I went down, instead of up, as was expected of me. He warned me not to go down, told me that I would run into demons. Unlike me, Slimspear is very religious. I cannot wait to tell him how wrong he was!"

There was one narrow door to the snowcastle, at the top of a long flight of icy steps. The white walls converged on both sides of the door, making whoever was on the steps an easy target.

"You had better stay below," Greylock warned. "It may take a few minutes for me to convince Slimspear that it is really me, and not a demon."

He bounded up the stairs, handling the slippery steps with an accustomed ease. At the top, he paused and knocked softly at the heavy wooden door set in the ice. At the last moment, he pulled the hood of his mountain cloak over his gray mane of hair. A small slit opened in one of the panels almost immediately and a frightened voice emerged. "Go away, demon!"

"Slimspear! Open up! It is I, Greylock. Hurry, let me in before someone else sees that I have come back."

"You do not fool me, demon. You could not be Greylock. The Gatekeepers say that only demons, and he who shall be their Deliverer, may return from below. Therefore, though you have taken the face and voice of my friend Greylock, you are a demon."

"Would a demon know the name Slimspear, or

that you have always been in love with my sister, Ardra, but were afraid to tell her? Or have you told others since I left?''

The panel snapped shut abruptly, and Greylock wondered if he had frightened his oldest friend away. Then the massive door opened timidly, grinding slowly, and the pale plump face of Mordref could be seen.

''Is it really you, Greylock?''

''Of course it's me!'' Greylock grabbed his friend by the shoulders and looked him in the eyes intently for several seconds. ''Do you really have any doubt?'' he said quietly.

Relief flooded Slimspear's face and he threw open the door. As he hugged the returned prince, Greylock motioned to the hidden Underworlders abruptly from behind his back. They hurried up the stairs, trying desperately to maintain their footing and their speed, the sight of the warm interior summoning them. Then they were through the open door.

Slimspear followed them through the windswept inner courtyard and into the small, cozy rooms within the stone walls at the end of the long outer corridors, staring at the two visitors in shock. All the color had drained from his face. The owner of the snowcastle belied by his appearance his name. He was anything but slim, and had received his nickname from Greylock by once vowing that he would someday be as slim as a spear. Now he looked as if he would never eat again.

''What is it, Slimspear?'' Greylock exclaimed, concerned by the intensity of his friend's reaction.

''I have failed!''

"What do you mean, Slimspear?"

"For generations beyond counting, my family has held Castle-Guardian, pledged to protect the High Plateau from demons. Now I have let two—no, three, for you must be one, too—into my country!" Greylock had removed his hood, revealing his silver hair. "Demons! I have failed the Tyrant, and my people."

"Nonsense, Slimspear," Greylock coaxed, as only friends can. "I have been to the Underworld. It is not full of demons. It is not anything like what the Gatekeepers say. . . ." Greylock realized suddenly that nothing he was saying was penetrating his friend's daze. Desperately he said, "Cheer up, Slimspear. How do you know I am not this Deliverer the Gatekeepers are always talking about?"

Though Greylock had tried to conceal his real wonderings behind this joke, Mordref saw through it, and glimpsed his concern.

"Of course! You are the Deliverer. You must be! I should have known."

The three spies relaxed at last, and fell into the soft chairs. They were safe until morning.

Later, Slimspear took his friend aside and broke the news of the Lady Silverfrost's coming marriage to the Steward Redfrock.

"I must speak to her!" he exclaimed. "Does she believe me dead?"

"No, Greylock," Slimspear said sadly. "You must not talk to her. You do not realize all that has happened since you left. The Steward's power has increased, and Silverfrost has given in to him. She is his completely now."

"I don't believe you!" Greylock denied what he

was hearing. "She hates Carrell Redfrock!"

"Silverfrost was never what you thought she was, Greylock. She has a weak will and is not worthy of you. It is time you realized that."

"Let us see what she says when I am Tyrant!" Greylock said, knowing she would come to him then—and not sure if he would take her.

Chapter Five

By early the following morning, the blizzard had passed and the skies were clear and blue. The two visitors from the Underworld, and the returning prince, stared at Godshome in awe from the Castle-Guardian's icetower. The three even peaks zigzagged across the horizon in white, crisp lines. The High Plateau stretched flat and even toward the mountain, in an almost perfect triangle. Other, smaller snowcastles dotted the plain, and two large snowcastles, with what looked to be a small village between them, sat on a huge Icemelt. Greylock identified the larger of the snowcastle's as Castle-Tyrant, his uncle's home; and the slightly smaller snowcastle as Castle-Steward. Around each of the snowcastles that were visible, was the disconcerting sight of green trees and brush, where the pockets of warmth called Icemelts sprouted from the snows.

Late into the night Greylock had discussed the matters of the realm with Slimspear. Little had changed, except that the Tyrant had grown more ill and even more oppressive, and that some of the rivals to his throne were coming out into the open in the jockeying for power. Chief among them was Greylock's enemy, Carrell Redfrock. It was a dangerous gambit, Greylock thought, while the Tyrant was still alive. Apparently, no one expected any of the sons or nephews to return, which was no surprise to Greylock.

Greylock reluctantly ended their awestruck reverie of Godshome. "We must hurry down and meet the others before anyone else is up and around."

The three spies slipped down the upper portions of the Gateway, almost running until they reached the rough, lower trails. Even then they made better time than they had on the way up, for Greylock had borrowed a pair of Talons from Slimspear. They met the men of the BorderKeep far down the mountain, stymied at the base of the first of the broken stretches. This was not as much progress as Greylock had hoped, but he restrained his impatience. It did not matter as long as they arrived while there was still daylight. He did not want to be caught with these men on Godshome at night; especially since their coming was to be a surprise.

As soon as they had gained entrance to his

uncle's snowcastle, he thought, victory was assured. The night before, Greylock had gone to the cellars of Castle-Guardian and made sure that the secret lava tube passage to Castle-Tyrant remained clear and unguarded. Greylock's unknown entrance would make even the Tyrant's own personal chambers vulnerable to the Underworld army, he believed.

Greylock hurried the men along the last stretch of road to Slimspear's snowcastle, past the Icemelts on the trail, glad that there was not any kind of storm. Even with the clear trails and good weather, they had been lucky not to lose any men to the mountain. Luckily they were not visible from the High Plateau at any point along the Gateway. The walls of the mountain's cliffs stretched up out of sight on one side, and an observer would have had to be well out over the edge of the plateau to see them. Only the protected portals of Castle-Guardian faced away from the plateau and toward the road, as was its function, and since its master believed Greylock to be the Deliverer himself, they were unobserved by enemy eyes.

Once the army was safely crowded within Castle-Guardian, Greylock left them in the courtyard and rushed up the icetower to survey the white plain of the plateau. Only at the sight of the calm, untroubled snows was he satisfied that they had not been seen. He wound down the stairs to where his followers waited, but instead of stopping, he continued on down the flight of stairs past them. He motioned for them to follow him, down into the darkened depths of the snowcastle. Giving each other anxious looks, the men of BorderKeep followed hesitantly.

The cellar must have been dug into the rock of the High Plateau itself, the wizard Moag thought. It was an impressive feat, and he thought it even more impressive when he realized that the base of the plateau was almost all lava stone, aside from the few inches of topsoil carefully accumulated in the few Icemelts. But the tunnels which lay concealed behind the huge kegs of icewater were natural; long spiraling lava tubes that worked their way down into the bowels of the mountain. Moag suspected that if they continued to take only the downward turns, they would reach the point where the earth melted, and firestone was created.

Greylock apparently did not intend to take this downward course, but instead led across the plateau diagonally to the Tyrant's snowcastle, through the well-traveled caves of his youth; and down a few he believed only he knew the way through.

Greylock gave every tenth man a torch and ushered the stilled and frightened company of soldiers into the yawning black cavern. When they hesitated again, he rushed forward to take the lead and was gratified to find yeoman Harkkor following. Greylock had never become lost in the caverns, though some of his childhood friends had not had such an easy time of it. He had always seemed to know where he was beneath the mountain, and where to turn next. Slimspear had never become so comfortable, and this time remained behind to keep a watch on their rear.

The air was cool and stuffy, yet the close atmosphere actually seemed to give the Underworlders a strange sense of warm safety after the blizzards they had endured. But as they descended deeper into the bewilderingly complex route of tunnels, the air became noticeably warmer, and the soldiers noticeably less comfortable with the warmth. They breathed easier when the path seemed to ascend once more, but then it dipped downward again at an alarming angle. Greylock did not answer their increasingly worried questions, and ignored their fear. They were safe, but he doubted he would ever be able to convince them of that.

Only the lava dust that covered the floor felt moist and cool. Sometimes the tunnel constricted suddenly and the way was blocked. Then they had to dig their way through, crawling through the narrow openings. Leading the troop with his hand extended over his head, Greylock called out the sudden dives and obstructions of the rough craggy roof. Since he was by far the tallest of the company, and yeoman Harkkor the broadest, no one should have cracked their heads. But occasionally one of the soldiers of the BorderKeep would cease to pay attention for a moment and would walk into the rock, creating a scalp wound that bled profusely, and which had to be bandaged. Before long, he noticed that the nervous troop was walking bent over in a stoop that rivaled Moag's.

Sometimes a crack in the roof would reveal daylight from above. The snow curved inward over these holes, dark blue and dripping steadily at their bases; pure white, with the sun shining through, on the top few inches. They could see from these glimpses how deep the snow was, but more importantly to Greylock, he guided them by these occasional markers of light. Sunlight streamed down into the dark caves, lighting the tunnels for hundreds of feet both ways. Sometimes, after traveling for long minutes in the dark, it was a shock to come across these spots of light and realize that it was still day outside.

As children, Greylock and Slimspear had defied their parents, as generations of children of the High Plateau had, and explored the endless caverns, until they knew every path to each other's castles, as well underground as they did above.

Still, the familiar paths sometimes seemed to shift on them if they were away from them for long—and Greylock had not been below for years.

The first change he noticed was a turn to the left that should have been to the right, and then a turn that should not have been there at all, and finally a long descent that did not appear as if it would ever end. At the bottom of this pit he was confronted by an unfamiliar fork in the path.

As Greylock hesitated, Moag noticed his puzzlement and distress and hurried over to him. "What is wrong, Greylock?" he asked in a low voice, not wanting the others to know they were lost, for he knew they would panic.

"This shouldn't be here! I have never seen this fork before, though it is on a level I am sure I have fully explored."

"Well, the choice is simple enough. One goes left and up; and one goes right, and down!"

"So it seems. But for how far?"

"Well, hurry up and choose, Greylock. Your army is getting nervous."

By now, the Lord High Mayor had realized something was wrong, and demanded to be told.

"My Familiar can find out which is the right one," he volunteered when it had been explained that they needed to go upward for some distance to reach Castle-Tyrant. Greylock could hear the claws of the rat as it scrambled down the Mayor's tall frame and disappeared into the dark. It was back within a few minutes.

"The right hand tunnel goes only downward," he announced when the rat was once more on his shoulder. "The left tunnel is the one we want," he said with certainty in his voice.

"Sometimes a tunnel will go downward for quite a distance before it angles up again," Greylock said doubtfully. "I think I will explore it a little further, just for the feel of it." He did not see the Mayor's face go pale as he darted into the same passage the rat had investigated.

This choice quickly began to angle further downward, as the rat had reported, and Greylock just as quickly changed his mind. He backtracked and found the others, who met him with nervous muttering, as well as a relieved look from the Mayor. But Greylock refused to show them any worry, and they continued to follow him, though very near to panic. The cave on the left seemed to be going in the proper direction, and he was still not suspicious; confident he could find his way out no matter what. Eventually, he reasoned, he would have to come across something he recognized.

The second tunnel also began to drop slightly, but took longer to reveal its course. The over-weight and out-of-shape soldiers were exhausted by now from this continual up and down movement, and when Greylock saw the yeomen also were sweating, but uncomplaining, he decided to give them rest before they were actually into the coming fight.

As the soldiers collapsed gratefully onto the dusty floor, breathing heavily and staring at each other in commiseration, Greylock took this time to slip away into the dark. Running back down the pitch black tunnel, with only a small torch for light, he backtracked for some distance to see if he could discover where he might have gone wrong. The troop's path was easily discernable by the turmoil they had created in the lava dust. The churned up tracks would be seen for many years to come, he thought, if no one happened along to disturb them. Yet, suddenly, these tracks came up against a solid rock wall! Greylock dropped to his knees and searched desperately for a seam at the base of the wall. They were in a trap!

It seemed impossible to Greylock that the old caves could have been tampered with. Secret passages and mysterious doors that closed after you had passed were the stuff of legends. But now he recognized where he had passed the old, well-traveled corridor—that was now blocked off and disguised by a false wall. There was no budging the stone slab.

There was only one person who could have engineered this—the Steward. Very well, Greylock thought, even Carrell Redfrock could not seal off all the caves. They would explore every tunnel; explore as long as they still lived. Above all, he must not let the others know of their danger!

"I remember now!" he announced loudly when he rejoined the others, though he doubted that he had fooled the magician and his granddaughter. "This was the right way all along. Now, it may get a little rough from here on out, but we are almost there. Stay together and keep an eye on me."

The passage actually started upward for a short way and Greylock had a sudden, wild hope that he might have somehow outmaneuvered the Steward. Then his hopes were dashed by an almost impossibly steep slope downward. Joining hands, they started to inch their way down. Greylock was encouraged to see side passages begin to appear. He declined to turn into any of them—guessing that the Steward would expect him to take these invitingly convenient exits.

Down they went into the mountain until the walls began to glow with an eerily red glow, and became too hot to touch. The men began to remove their outer garments, careful not to accidentally brush their hands against the steaming rock. Their surface discipline was finally beginning to crack, and Greylock began to hear muttered curses and threats behind his back. As these became louder, Greylock was made aware of yeoman Harkkor's stolid presence as he jostled him, smiling encouragingly. But the soldiers depended on him, now more than ever, to lead them out again, so he was safe. As long as they still think I can lead them out, he thought.

By now Greylock was sure that he had gone further into the mountain than even Steward Redfrock could have predicted and allowed for. He at last began considering a turn away from the approaching heat, though all the side tunnels also appeared to descend. But suddenly they emerged on a natural balcony, high in the side of a vast deep cavern.

The pit was brimming with molten lava. They watched in awe as a huge globule of firestone sprang violently from the shimmering pool and seemed to hang before their eyes, larger than the perch on which they stood and radiating an intense heat, before it dropped slowly, majestically back into the pool. At several points along the sides of the cliff below them, rivers of bright firestone flowed from lava falls into the bright lake. This was the source of the High Plateau's heat, Greylock thought, the source of its Icemelts, and its life.

At first they were too stunned to move, but within a few seconds the intense heat had driven them back, covering their faces with their hands and the folds of their cloaks. They did not cease their retreat until they had gone around the first of the abrupt turns. The steaming walls now seemed relatively cool, and they leaned against them, catching their breath and feeling as if their lungs had been seared.

Without a word, the subdued soldiers followed Greylock into one of the side passages. All of them seemed to have become unnaturally sensitive to the hellish pit and knew instantly when they were nearing it again. For a while, it seemed as if every choice led back to it again, but because of their new awareness of temperature they began making slow progress toward the cooler portions of the underground network.

Eventually the maze started to lead upward at last, and Greylock excitedly recognized a few marks on the walls. He suddenly knew where the path was leading—and it was where he wanted to go. He led quickly from that point.

● ● ●

The huge cavern beneath Castle-Tyrant was the most public and familiar of all the lava tubes. Lying near the village, many celebrations had taken place within it over the years, safe from the cruel mountain blizzards. Natural skylights spotted the enormous roof and the cavern was well lit—almost blinding to the men entering suddenly from the dark caverns below. Blackened stumps and half-burned logs marked where bonfires had been lit to give some warmth, and potholes lined the walls where children had dug into the soft dirt.

No celebrations or festivals had been allowed for some time, apparently not since the Tyrant had first fallen ill. Litter spotted the eroding footprints in the dust, and crude ladders and ropes hung forlornly from the roof. This traditional gathering spot had always been untended and natural, but now Greylock had to wrinkle his nose distastefully at the smell of garbage. The ancient pit had become a refuse heap, a dumping place for all the trash and slop of the High Plateau. Even the wind whistling through the gaping holes in the roof could not take away the awful odor.

Straight ahead of them were the beckoning broad stairs carved into the walls, leading to the entrance of Castle-Tyrant. The army rushed toward them, anxious to confront a human enemy at last—and Greylock was at their head, eager to fling his escape at the Steward Redfrock. His feet had barely touched the first step when a roaring wind flowed down the stairs, throwing Greylock violently backward onto the earth. The torch was plucked from his hand and snuffed out.

The torches in the hands of the others sputtered only briefly in defiance of the gale before they, too, winked out. For a few more stunned seconds, the daylight continued to stream down the holes in the roof, the muffled glow catching the disturbed particles of dust briefly in its light. Then platforms of rock slammed down over the holes with a frightening thud, knocking huge fragments from the roof down upon the terrified Keepsmen.

A ghostly voice filled the chamber, and Greylock could recognize the strained rasp of his uncle's throat. The voice must have been magnified by echo chambers somewhere in the staircase, he thought. All of the men of the BorderKeep could hear the frightening words of that whispery voice.

"Now, I have you, demons! Did you think you could surprise me; that I would not have every entrance to my kingdom thoroughly guarded? Or did you believe I would be fooled by the guise of my nephew? Stay where you are, demons, and rot! There is no escape from this prison!"

Greylock realized that his uncle's trap had succeeded where the Steward Redfrock's had not.

Chapter Six

Greylock learned quickly the fickleness of his allies, to his dismay. It did not take more than a few seconds of total darkness for the men of the BorderKeep to panic. Most of them had never before been plunged into a world where they could make no light to fill the darkness without the flames being blown out by another of the magical gusts of wind.

When he had finally had enough of the Keepsmen's wails and of the Lord High Mayor's recriminations, Greylock called out in his quick temper for Moag. His voice was drowned out twice before he angrily bellowed above the furor. The startled soldiers ceased pleading to their gods for a few shocked moments, as if they expected him to reassure them that there was a way out. Then it was past, and the first of the Underworlders began to shout again, with the others quickly following his example. But not before Moag was able to feel his way over to Greylock, his bony strong fingers searching for a calm and unmoving figure among the frightened soldiers, and knowing instantly when he had found Greylock.

"You must get us out of here, wizard!" Greylock demanded desperately, knowing that he was being unreasonable.

"There is little I can do, Prince Greylock," the old man answered. "Did you know that your uncle has the power? A strong earth-magic, I believe. We are sealed in by the physical, and we are sealed in by the magical, as well."

"I was a fool to challenge my uncle." Greylock finally allowed his doubts to emerge. "He has beaten me every step of the way; just as he has always outwitted the Steward Redfrock and every other opponent. If only I could speak with him, and tell him what the Underworld is really like!"

"No, you were not a fool. You just picked the wrong army, Greylock. We should have gone to Trold. Then we wouldn't have had to skulk underground."

"At least you could give us some light, old man!" Greylock said angrily to the old man's carping.

"You realize that a fire will use up air?"

"If we do not have light, we shall never escape anyway! We may live longer in the dark, but the end will be just as certain."

Moag did not answer, and Greylock could hear the sounds of the wizard bending over and his hands scurrying along the ground. Then he saw the light of the unnatural blue flame of magic nestled in a small pile of rubbish that the old man had apparently collected. Then the flame caught, and Greylock blinked at a clean white light that was not blown out but grew—until at last the shapes of the Keepsmen were illuminated and their shadows were sent swiftly climbing the walls.

Before Greylock had a chance to stop them, the soldiers had spread this one fire with joyful cries to a dozen other fires lit about the chamber. Those men who weren't clustered around these reassuring flames, glorying in the light, were off gathering bits of burnable trash.

Luckily, Greylock thought, the fires did not seem to be giving off much smoke and he reasoned that putting out some of the fires would cause more smoke, and more complaining, than could be endured. Besides, he hoped, there had to be *some* air entering the chamber through the porous lava stone.

The Lord High Mayor had come to join Greylock and the wizard by the original fire. The rat sat unconcernedly on the Mayor's shoulder, and Greylock thought with a shudder that the Familiar could live indefinitely in the cave, feeding off the trash. Soon there would be even fresher food for it. Greylock doubted the animal would decline the temptation of dining on his former master. Greylock could not see that the thoughts of the Lord High Mayor were running in much the same vein, as Tarelton wondered if he had been

132

betrayed and abandoned.

It was Lord High Mayor Tarelton who first noticed that Mara was missing.

At first, Greylock was not really worried by the absence. After all, where could she go? he thought. He remembered seeing her just before the torches had gone out, therefore she had to be in the chamber somewhere. But soon his search became frantic when she did not turn up, no matter how hard they looked, and his shouts echoed off the roof and walls. She had vanished into thin air.

• • •

When the Underworlders had first entered the cavern below the Castle-Tyrant, Mara's eyes had been caught by the unmistakable gleam of Glyden flashing near one of the walls. Thinking vaguely of how nice it would be to present her grandfather with a gift of Glyden, and remembering Greylock's tales of its plentitude on the High Plateau, she was drawn toward one of the children's excavations along the wall. This hole was quite deep, and just wide enough for a young boy—or a small woman. At the bottom flashed the gilded object, but she could still not see what it was.

While the others were absorbed in the sights of the cave, and just beginning their dash toward the stairs, she jumped in idly, knowing that she was being foolish and hoping that the loose earth would not cave in on her. When the child's tunnel ended after only a few yards, and she found nothing, she shrugged at her foolishness and began to back out, hoping that the others had not left her behind in her brief sojourn.

But backing out did not prove as easy as entering had been, and she felt herself squeezed by the roof, whereas on her way in she had not felt it at all. Soon she was sure that her inward passage had dropped enough earth from the roof to obstruct her exit. Half cursing her stupidity in searching for Glyden, when if she had waited as she had always told her grandfather to do she would have gotten all the Glyden she wanted, and half in panic, she struggled to turn around. This proved too much for the roof, which had never been meant to contain an adult, and it collapsed behind her, filling the hole with dust and drawing from her a coughing fit which threatened to bring down the rest of the tunnel at any moment.

Trying desperately to maintain her presence of mind, Mara began calling out; at first for her grandfather, and then in more panic, for Greylock, and finally with frightened shrieks, for help from anyone who could hear her. But no sounds penetrated her tomb, except for one loud thud that again threatened to bring down the wall of the tunnel. After a moment she thought she could hear a ghostly laughter, but then decided she must have imagined it. She did not realize that the others had also just been sealed within a deadly trap.

The tears began to streak down through her dust-covered cheeks and the dirt collected at the corners of her lips. Her blond hair fell over her face, but she did not flick it aside for it did not matter—she could see nothing. Not for several minutes did she think of using her magic. She had so stubbornly refused to summon any help from

134

magic in the past that the habit had never become part of her thinking. Even now she was reluctant to use it. She tried to remember the spell she had used once before, with astonishing results, up on the mountain pass. Her eyes closed and she summoned the hated and unwanted power, but though she could feel it just beyond her grasp, she discovered as her grandfather already had above her, that she was constrained by a power greater than hers.

Left with only one recourse, she began carefully, then more frantically, to dig upward. She shoveled the earth behind her harder and faster as the seconds passed, but the air she was breathing was the same air, she realized, that had been trapped with her long minutes ago. She was breathing it in great gasps now, but this did not seem to relieve the ache in her lungs. Soon she was no longer paying any attention to the direction she was digging, but just grabbing handfuls of the earth, the dirt that came away easiest, and it fell about her like rain.

It seemed ironic to her that, as a Witch of the Winds, she had always stubbornly refused to use her power over this element; now despite her willingness at last to use her magic, she was about to die of suffocation!

Suddenly, she realized to her horror that she had ceased to go upward at all, but had settled for following the soft earth almost directly forward. Her second shock was that when she proceeded to correct this direction she was met by solid rock. She fell back into the hole sobbing in frustration, ready at that moment to give up. She clawed futilely and pathetically at the wall, the dirt now causing pain under her fingernails, and to her astonishment, her hand suddenly went through the earth and encountered air on the other side!

For a few minutes, she did not bother to enlarge the hole, but settled for breathing deeply the wisps of fresh air it tantalizingly provided. Then she pulled at the earth with renewed vigor and it came away easily, enlarging the hole to her satisfaction. She called out twice, but when no answer came back, she realized that she must have emerged into another of the endless caves. But at that moment life seemed good, if only because it provided cool, sweet air—never mind that it was just as dark as before and that she had no idea where she was.

She soon realized that it was not quite as pitch black as she first thought. There seemed to be a pinpoint of light, that could barely be perceived by the eye, visible perhaps only because there was no other light to compete with it. If she glanced away from the dot of light for even a moment, she could believe that she had imagined it. But it stayed there, unmoving, to be appreciated if she stared at it long enough, and she decided it was real.

She crawled out of her own little cave, which had almost been her grave, and walked cautiously toward the prick of light, her hands extended blindly. From the echoing sound of her footsteps, she realized that she was in another giant enclosure, at least as big as the one she had just left, and as she neared she saw that the light was high up on its wall, a square doorway of light that barely illuminated a flight of narrow steps. Unafraid, she mounted the staircase and passed through the shimmering portal.

On the other side was a simple stone platform, flanked by two other staircases leading down a few steps until they were blocked by massive wooden doors; and one staircase that led up out of sight, lit by torches. She skipped down to one of the doors and tugged, then pushed at it. As she had suspected, it would not budge. With determination in her young face, she marched up the long flight of stairs.

At the top of the long straight stairway, she was confronted by another of the huge doors. Behind it she could barely hear a great bustle; the clanking of pots and pans, the shouts and laughter of women. This door was unlocked, and daring to push it open a crack, Mara saw what she immediately assumed to be many serving women, moving about a steaming kitchen with good-natured and agile speed, despite their bulk. One by one, giant trays of food were lifted with grunts and carried from the room on their shoulders, until at last it was empty, of both food and servants. It certainly did not seem as if they were concerned about the fighting, she thought wonderingly. Where were the others!

Cautiously, but licking her lips hungrily, Mara stepped into the room. A few scraps of meat had been left on a long wooden slab, a huge block of wood that served as both a table and a cutting board. Dozens of knives were stuck negligently into its scoured and stained surface. Not knowing that she was stealing the food of the Steward's Familiar, she grabbed at the food and ate it hungrily. Then she began to explore the snowcastle. At the last moment, she plucked a knife from its stubborn hold in the wood.

On the other side of the wide swinging doors through which the serving women had exited, Mara heard the loud noises of dining and triumphant laughter. But to the right, she spied a narrow staircase that seemed to follow the path she had taken to the kitchen, and she darted over to it, almost as to an old friend.

Many doors and landings led off these stairs, but she went on to the top, not knowing what else to do and thinking vaguely that she would find a vantage point there that would afford a view. At the top, though, there was only a narrow and dark door without a landing. Reaching up from a few steps below the door, she opened and peered in.

It was a sparse room; a small room with no windows. Only a huge stone bed filled one end of the room, and the rest was bare stone. But what she noticed most was the cold. It felt like icicles were being thrust into her hands and face.

Yet, despite the freezing temperature, an old, old man was lying on the hard frame of the bed, asleep with his mouth open, and very near death. Suddenly, the ancient red-lidded eyes in an almost blue face opened, and black eyes pierced her even more than the frigid cold of the room. Only when those eyes changed suddenly into a deceptive merriment did she recognize his features. This old man had to be Greylock's uncle, the Tyrant of the High Plateau!

"Come in, demongirl," his voice cracked. "I am not so ill that I imagine you, nor am I so ill that I cannot defend myself against any demon. It does not matter anyway, for I have already entered the

Deathroom, and once here I may not leave. Come in, and sit by me on my death bed. Tell me of Greylock. Why has he returned?"

Mara was not fooled by the old man's twinkling eyes. She had heard too many stories of the hard life on the High Plateau, and of the cruel leader who had ruled it for so long. Shivering, she sat on the very end of the bed, on the edge, ready to flee at any moment. "He has come to take his rightful place as your heir. And to tell you that you have been wrong about the Underworld and the Gateway."

"He has come to take my place!" The Tyrant would have roared, had his voice been able, but the strain in his face was just as effective. Then the old man laughed strangely. "I hope he does take my place—better him than that treacherous Steward. But he must win by fighting for it, as I did. First he must kill the Steward Redfrock, for I am already dead. He will not find that easy."

Mara was confused by the sick man's sudden shifts of mood. The Tyrant is mad! she thought with a sudden insight. She fingered the carving knife concealed under the folds of her cloak.

"Tell my nephew, if he lives, that I am proud of him. I thought none of my heirs would challenge me. They all accepted exile and death meekly. Perhaps the time has come at last when the Gateway can be opened again."

"I will tell him."

Now the black eyes were changing again, and the face was filling with the rage that was the curse of the royal family.

"Demon!" he hissed, as if he had just noticed

her, as perhaps one part of him had. "How did you escape my trap? Guards! Guards! Bring me Thunderer, that I may destroy this creature."

Mara dropped the kitchen knife clattering onto the stone floor, and fled from the room.

● ● ●

"I thought you said you could not use your magic to escape!" Greylock was angrily accusing the wizard in the cave below Castle-Tyrant.

"I can't!" Moag answered in a defensive and bewildered voice. "If I can't use my power, at your command, neither can she—not alone. Her natural power may be greater than mine, and I have often suspected just that, but that power is still untrained."

The Lord High Mayor had followed the two in their frantic search, at first bemused but not really concerned. Now he was beginning to have second thoughts about the Steward's intentions. He whispered into his Familiar's ear, and the rat left his master's shoulder for the second time, using his claws to scramble down his master's chest and dropping the last few feet to the floor of the chamber. Then it disappeared into the rubbish and the shadows.

As the others continued to search and argue fruitlessly, Mayor Tarelton made himself comfortable in the soft dust near the fire and waited for his Familiar to return. The rat came back eventually licking its snout, having apparently dined while it was gone, and scurried up to its comfortable perch on the shoulder of its master. As the rat reported what it had found in its own search, the Lord High Mayor casually rose to his feet and went looking for Greylock and the wizard. He found them out in the dark, still arguing heatedly.

"I know where she is—or where she was last," he said, interrupting their worried discussion.

"What do you mean?" Greylock asked, fearing the worst.

Moag only stared at the Mayor in shock, his face growing suddenly pale. He put both of his hands over his face and grew very still. The other two stopped curiously, and watched silently, knowing that this was not a reaction to the news, but something deeper and internal. Then the old man seemed to recover, as if he had reassured himself somehow about Mara's fate.

"She is alive, yet she is not here," he announced.

"How could that be . . ." Greylock began, but the wizard shushed him.

"Show us where she disappeared," he commanded the Mayor.

By fits and starts, for the Mayor continually had to stop and listen to the Familiar's instructions, he led them toward one of the cavern walls. The light was dim here, but all could see the caved-in remains of a child's excavation to which he pointed, a few yards from the blank wall. Now it was Greylock's turn to grow pale. He dropped into the shallow hole and began digging in panic at the freshly caved-in earth.

"She is alive, I tell you," Moag said calmly above him. "Yet she is not with us here in this cave."

Greylock ceased his digging and stared at the

wizard. "What do you mean? What are you two talking about?"

"She has found a way out, Greylock," Moag appeared to be confused. "Yet not by magic."

"How can that be?" Even as he said this, Greylock quickly realized the only possibility.

Now the Lord High Mayor joined in the hopeful speculation. "Perhaps this tunnel leads to another cave and she was able to dig her way out!" he said excitedly.

"If she has done that, by herself, then together we can dig another tunnel!"

Many of the men who had followed them, willing to help in the search, seized at this hope and began digging. But others seemed to have already given up and sat together in lackadaisical bunches, seemingly grateful just for the next breath. The fires were flickering and sputtering, and though more rubbish was being thrown onto them, the flames were a pathetic remnant of the roaring fires of a few minutes before. Even as Greylock watched the dwindling energy of his men, the first of the fires went out, and then another. Black smoke spiraled upward to meet the unyielding rock of the cave roof, and then filled the chamber with an acrid, choking fog. Increasingly, they could not even see the smoke they were choking on.

Greylock saw that it would be a race between suffocation and escape. He directed his men along the line of the old tunnel, thinking that it would be easier digging. But they were constantly confronted by huge stones, impossible to budge. They could never tell when a rock was first uncovered whether it was only a few inches across and could be moved, or whether it would turn out to be frustratingly deep in its grip on the earth. They wasted a good deal of precious time and energy on these hopelessly mired stones, until finally Greylock ordered them to dig around them, even if it appeared to be a roundabout way of reaching the wall.

At last they were under the original wall, and perhaps close to freedom. Yet, so near to their goal, the Keepsmen began to slow down considerably. Greylock saw to his frustration that progress was coming to a standstill, and he himself had dropped into an exhausted crouch, as if standing were too much of an effort, and he was breathing so heavily that he could hear himself. He could not ask the Keepsmen to do more, he thought, for they were as aware of the danger of inaction as he was. They were so close! Yet it was obvious they were going to lose their race with the rapidly dwindling supply of air.

The last of the fires winked out, and Greylock heard the wizard mutter, "How I wish I had my granddaughter's power over the wind!"

Then no one said a word, for to speak would have been too much of an effort.

Mara fled down the stairs from the Deathroom, her feet flying over three steps at a time, and she felt as if she were falling into a deep, great well. Every stone in the wall seemed to leap up past her, brightly lit. But she was still in control when she reached the junction of the kitchen again.

At the bottom of these steps, Mara was suddenly confronted by one of the inhabitants of the snowcastle. A young girl, with dark hair and eyes, and a plump cheerful face stared back, as Mara's eyes darted about desperately for an escape. As far as she could see, this girl was her single obstacle; but the old Tyrant's enraged voice was still drifting down the halls, and guards could happen along at any moment. She brushed by the strange girl, who grabbed ineffectually at her arm.

"No, wait!" the other girl cried. "I am Greylock's sister!"

"Ardra?" Mara stopped and turned, immediately seeing the resemblance to Greylock in this plump girl.

"Is it true? Is Greylock with those others?"

"Do you know where he is?" Mara asked anxiously.

"The Tyrant has trapped them below. Follow me! I know where they are, but I do not know how we can free them!"

Ardra took the steps as quickly as Mara had done. Their pursuers would not dare to follow, Mara thought. They would undoubtedly be constrained by their own bulky armor and by the steepness of the stairs. They would need to take each step carefully, one at a time. But it still would not leave them with much time to free Greylock and her grandfather, if what Ardra had hinted was true.

Ardra led her back to that same landing she had entered from the darkness of the caves. To the right was the door which led back to the chamber she had just emerged from—so she knew they were not there. And the left-hand door led away from the direction she had known the others to be last.

Only the door directly ahead of them could be hiding the captives, she thought, and Ardra confirmed this suspicion by pointing at the giant barrier.

"But it is locked! I have already tried to open it!"

Ardra could only shrug helplessly. She looked back up the stairs in alarm at the sound of armor.

Mara began to examine the huge oaken door, with its braces of hardened leather and bolts of brass, for some way to opening it; first with her hands, and then with her mind. Her senses quickly told her that she would never be able to force the door open physically, and the same barrier that had confronted her magical powers before was still intact, and actually seemed concentrated at this very door. But it was a simple, if very strong, trap spell, designed only to keep men within its grip, not to keep others out. On this side of the door she was no longer constrained by the spell, and it would not be a hindrance to her powers.

She knew her grandfather could have opened the door with a minimum of fuss and with great finesse. If he had been there, the portal would no doubt have simply popped open at his command. But she did not have the time and the patience to work with such care. She summoned the raw power she had always known she possessed and directed it at the wooden barrier.

The door exploded with killing force, sending deadly shards down both sides of the passage. But the very force of her magic wind continued to protect Ardra and her from the fragments, sending them glancing off them in mid-air and burying the splinters in the walls and floors.

It was dark and quiet beyond, and the air smelled stale and sickly. Mara sent fresh air from the halls behind her whistling down into the black hole beyond the door. Then, and only then, did they dare enter.

Behind the two girls, though still far above, came the clattering of weapons as the snowcastle's guards realized where Mara was at last and what she had done, and hurried to stop her before she had freed her companions. But it took much longer, as she had hoped it would, for the soldiers in their bulky armor to negotiate the narrow steps. They did not dare take them at the speed with which Ardra and she had escaped. Indeed, if she was not mistaken, some of the racket she had heard was the sound of one of them who didn't make it falling. She hoped that the careless soldier would bring others down in his fall. To help them along, she sent the wind whistling down the narrow twisting corridor once more.

The steep stairs continued from the landing down into darkness, but the walls gradually fell away on both sides, and she realized from the echo of their steps that she was once again within a vast cavern. But where were the skylights? Even more important, where were Greylock and Moag? She was certain, even without Ardra's assurance, that this was the same cave in which she had left the others.

Timidly at first, then realizing that it made no difference if anyone heard her, she shouted as loud as she could and Ardra's hesitant voice was added to hers. Their cries seemed to shock the atmosphere of the tomb, as if only whispers were meant to be spoken here, and how dare they break the ancient silence! But presently Mara thought she could hear a muffled answer from somewhere within the cavern, from the far side—and then she was sure that she heard several weak shouts.

Once beyond the light of the door, she tripped and fell once or twice in her hurry to reach the others, and Ardra helped her up. Summoning the blue flame that she had seen her father call forth so many times, and which was a physical manifestation of her magical powers, Mara cupped it in the palm of her hands. It did not glow as strongly as she would have wished and she realized with a fright that she had just about exhausted her magical powers this day, as well as her body's resources. She had wasted too much of it on the opening of the door, she realized, and now she was feeling a fatigue that was completely unfamiliar to her. Before, her problem had always been the other way around. Sometimes, for instance, she had felt she would burst with the malignant and destructive force of magic if she did not expend some of the awful power within her—a power she had been granted, but had neither asked for nor wanted. And now she had to admit to herself that she had experienced a kind of satisfaction in at last doing what her grandfather had always insisted she was capable of, but which she had stubbornly resisted.

Before they had explored half of the cave, the muffled cries of amazement and joy they had heard after the bursting of the door grew stronger.

Then Greylock stumbled into Mara's blue light.

He appeared dazed and at first did not even seem to recognize her. She left her blue flame hanging in mid-air and reached for his shoulders, shaking him violently.

"Greylock, you must prepare! The Tyrant's guards are coming, this minute! What is wrong with you?"

"Mara? Ardra?" Slowly, the truth of his unexpected freedom—and his new danger—filled his awareness. By now other men were gathering around the dangling blue flame, like moths in the light of a torch.

"Quickly!" he shouted at last. "We must escape before they seal us in again!"

More than anything else could have, this threat seemed to alert the dazed soldiers of their danger, Revived suddenly, they bounded toward the beckoning square of light that was their only escape route—just as the light was blocked by the figure of a warrior. The guards had reached the landing just as the Underworld army surged toward it.

The battle that followed was a bloody struggle that horrified Greylock. All his plans of conquest had depended on surprise—but they had been the ones who were surprised. Only the lucky escape of Mara had saved them from being sealed forever in a tomb beneath the Castle-Tyrant. Now evenly matched and determined armies confronted each other on the small stone landing under the snow-castle. In this strange battle, only a few men could fight at the same time, while the others watched the life and death struggle in dread, and waited to take the place of the fallen. Only the presence of the yeomen of the BorderKeep such as Harkkor saved the Underworld army from being annihilated, for only they could withstand the assault for long. There were no survivors on that awful battleground. All who entered were slain. Only the length of time they managed to stay alive changed.

There was no danger now of the door being replaced, for it was shattered completely by the magic wind, and the Underworld army would never allow the other army to seal them in again, unless each and every soldier of the Underworld army was dead or dying. But Greylock could almost imagine that the narrow corridor would be impassable from the fallen men, for the bodies piled up between the legs of the fighters. The walls, and steps for many yards around, were red with their blood.

At last Greylock ordered a tentative retreat, ready to rush forward again if the snowcastle's army tried to seal them in again. As he hoped, the Tyrant's men followed them into the chamber. This was the kind of battle he liked, where skill could save a soldier, and only his own mistakes would cost him his life. He guessed that the Tyrant's guards also preferred this kind of death to the nightmarish slaughter on the landing.

Moag had cast his blue light high into the cave and let it grow, with the help of his granddaughter, until it illuminated every corner of the vast cave. It seemed that neither army would surrender or retreat in this twilight battle, and that one or the other would be destroyed to the last man. A few of the men Greylock faced appeared surprised at the sight of him, and their eyes would open slightly, and their guard would drop. Greylock did not wish to take advantage of these sudden doubts, but nevertheless dispatched them without mercy. Others seemed to fight with renewed vigor at the moment of recognititon, believing that it was a demon with whom they dueled.

But the battle's inevitable end could be seen early. Unless something could save the army of Underworlders, they were doomed. Though the forces had seemed evenly matched at the first, Greylock quickly realized that his uncle could call on all the royal snowcastles, and all the common snowcastles that owed him allegiance, for reinforcements. Despite the Lord High Mayor's claims of the prowess of his soldiers and the indulgences he had lavished on them, they were not equal, man for man, to the soldiers of the High Plateau, trained by years of blood-feuding. The yeoman farmers, though sturdy and determined, lacked the training of constant battle that seasons an army. If only he could get close to his uncle, Greylock thought. He would not try to convince the old man this time. No feeling—not pity, or loyalty— nothing would stay his hand!

Always before the old Tyrant had appeared at every battlefield, summoning his strength to enjoy one more glimpse of carnage. No doubt if the man could still wield a sword, he would have done that, too. His uncle must be very ill indeed, Greylock thought, not to be here now exhorting his men to further bloodshed in his royal name.

The Steward's staff descended three times, its iron base striking the hard rock of the steps with a screeching, piercing sound that rose above the sounds of battle. The men of both armies looked up, astonished that this strange old man, with a black crow on his shoulder, staring out into space and waiting silently for the fighting to subside, would dare to stop their war. Wondering how long the Steward had been standing there, hoping for the death of his rival, before he had become impatient enough to signal for silence, Greylock —without taking his eyes off the royal Steward —waved for his men to cease fighting. When the men of the Underworld lowered their arms, the soldiers of the High Plateau ceased their strife as well.

Like an ancient teacher who no longer cared if any of his pupils was still there to hear him, the Steward Redfrock waited until there was absolute silence and attention before he spoke. Then he boomed with an astonishing force for a man so slender and frail, until Greylock remembered that such official announcements had been his duty, as the Tyrant's messenger and advisor, for many years.

"The Tyrant is dead!"

This brought a murmur from the assembly, and a few cheers from the men of the BorderKeep, and Greylock frowned at them as the Steward intoned.

"The throne of the Tyrant is now open! The Gatekeepers wish to speak with the one who claims to be the nephew of the Tyrant Ironclasp, the demon known as Greylock. The Gatekeepers call upon him to end this bloodshed until the manner of succession is decided—peacefully."

Greylock hesitated at this seemingly generous offer. He knew that as long as he was considered a demon he would have less chance with the

151

Gatekeepers than he would by fighting. But the men of the High Plateau would fight just as fervently for the Gatekeepers as they had for the old Tyrant, until the new Tyrant was named, and the ending would be the same—the elimination of the Underworld army. They were within the Gatekeepers' grasp, and under their brief mercy. Greylock knew the Gatekeepers to be no kinder to their enemies than the old Tyrant had been. If there was one Council Greylock would prefer to avoid in deciding the question, it was his old teachers, and old foes, the priests of the Gateway.

Both armies parted for him expectantly and curiously, which decided him. He could not allow the killing to go on in his name, as he had once accused his uncle of doing. He must face the Gatekeepers and somehow convince them of his identity. It would not be easy, for no one knew better than he how dogmatic they could be.

He sheathed his replica of Thunderer and let himself be escorted by Carrell Redfrock, who turned with a sweep of his scarlet robes and led the way up the stairs with an imperial hauteur worthy of the Tyrant Ironclasp himself. The men behind them in the cavern followed them, reluctantly mingling with each other at the narrow portals of the staircase into the snowcastle.

Greylock was not fooled by Redfrock's seeming lack of concern over who was to be Tyrant. The old soldier would like everyone to believe that he cared only that the precious protocol be fulfilled; but Greylock knew that Carrell Redfrock was still his greatest rival and barrier to his uncle's throne, even after the succession was decided one way or the other.

Once a Tyrant was named by the Gatekeepers, he would then become a fair target for the intrigues and feuds of the Court and the Castle-Tyrant that characterized the royal family. Greylock's uncle had been unusual in the longevity of his reign, and unusual in his repressiveness and brutality, eliminating those most likely to threaten his rule—his own family.

At the top of the staircase, the Steward turned left toward the room where Mara had heard the sounds of dining earlier. Beyond was a room large enough to accommodate many of the soldiers of both armies, and the double stone thrones at one end of the room showed that it was the castle's Court. Waiting grimly before an enormous fireplace opposite the cold thrones were a dozen of the brown-robed and white-haired priests of the Gateway. They were old only because they allowed themselves the kind of age that they denied to everyone else but the Tyrant and the Steward. Greylock suspected that there were practical as well as religious reasons for the harsh and unforgiving penalties of the Gatekeepers. The population never seemed to rise above—never was allowed to rise above—the numbers that had existed when the society had first become stable hundreds of years ago. Greylock also suspected that this was the reason so many sought to become Gatekeepers or Tyrant or Steward; the peaceful seeking priesthood, the more warlike seeking the throne, and the cunning seeking the Stewardship. Yet all went without complaint when their time came to seek the cold comfort of the gods.

Most of the Gatekeepers were staring unhappily into the flames of the huge fire, stoked to an almost unbearable temperature, when the Steward announced Greylock, and a few of them did not look up even then. Greylock followed their gaze and saw the lump of molten Glyden deep within, with jewels lying like blackened cinders around it. Only the blade of Thunderer had endured the intense heat of the flames. It was hard for Greylock to believe that anyone would have subjected the ancient weapon and badge of office to the hot coals. Only the Steward could have done that with such impunity, and then only at the Tyrant's command! Ironclasp could not have been in his right mind, Greylock thought, to have allowed such a thing—or perhaps he had allowed Carrell Redfrock to convince him, for it was the Steward who had the most to gain from the destruction of the family heirloom.

It was Keyholder, the most venerable of the Gatekeepers, and Greylock's teacher, who addressed him first.

"Welcome, Greylock. Come forward so that we may see you."

Encouraged that his old teacher had not used the word demon, Greylock came forward awkwardly until he was close enough for the old priest to reach out a scrawny arm and grab him. The bright birdlike eyes searched Greylock's face intently before letting go the painful grip.

"You appear to be Prince Greylock . . .I do not believe that a demon would look such as you. But you must understand, my boy, that we must be sure. There is no test we can go by. This has never

154

happened before! Only Thunderer could have decided, for no demon could have possessed or even held onto the sacred blade. But your uncle has burned it! How do we decide?''

Though he had wielded the copy of Thunderer during the battle, Greylock had since sheathed the blade, and until now had forgotten it. Apparently, the sight of Thunderer in his hands had not yet been reported to the Gatekeepers. Hesitating for only a moment, and wondering if he was not perhaps making his situation worse, he drew the replica from its crude sheathe.

The Gatekeepers gasped when Greylock had removed entirely the makeshift gray covering from Thunderer.

"Demon!" he heard one of them hiss, just as he had feared. "You do not fool us!"

"It is impossible!" Redfrock objected. "A fake! I saw the Tyrant throw the blade into the fire myself!"

"Did you, Carrell Redfrock?" Greylock said, knowing it would make no difference in the outcome. "Mara saw my uncle on his deathbed. Did he leave the Deathroom to destroy Thunderer?" Without knowing it, he had scored a point, for all the Gatekeepers knew how unlikely it was that the old Tyrant would leave the Deathroom once entering it, for they knew him to be a devout man in his last days.

"Let me see it," Keyholder demanded. "Let me have it!"

Almost reluctantly, Greylock handed it over. The old priest would surely see that it was an eleborate, if magical, fake, and then he would denounce Greylock as a demon.

"I do not understand it!" Keyholder exclaimed. Greylock had never seen his old teacher's composure break before, even in the face of his most obnoxious student's most serious provocations. Now he was obviously bewildered and mystified. "This is Thunderer! The real Thunderer! I recognize the markings."

This announcement instantly changed the atmosphere in the room, and Greylock could almost feel the threat of violence which had surrounded him lift. He realized with a surging relief that the people of the High Plateau were not aware of the kind of magic the wizard Moag had employed to create this blade.

Yet that did not explain to him the startling similarities between the real and the fake. Or was it fake? How could the markings have been reproduced? Respectful glances were being cast in his direction as one by one the other Gatekeepers examined the blade and verified Keyholder's identification. Then came the words Greylock had never thought he would hear spoken, but had fought so hard to hear.

"We have decided that you are truly the person we knew as Greylock," Keyholder announced. "You possess the proper identification of your office. The sword you bear is Thunderer—a sign of your acceptance by the gods. You are the true successor to the throne! You are the Tyrant of the High Plateau."

Keyholder came forward—smiling, Greylock was astounded to see—and led him to one of the stone thrones. Greylock seated himself uneasily and wondered what he should say to the audience, as they eyed him curiously.

"My first command as Tyrant is. . . ." The Steward Redfrock must have guessed what that command would be, for he moved with a suddenness that surprised even his Familiar, perched on his shoulder. As Redfrock moved toward the wall, only a few feet away, the black crow was unwittingly launched into the air to circle above the surprised audience in the Court chamber, cawing loudly in distress. The Steward must have positioned himself carefully when he had first entered the Court, for after a few quick hand movements behind a tapestry, the wall slid aside and he slipped through. Before anyone could react, the wall had already slid shut again, leaving the tapestry billowing in the brief gust of its passage. The soldiers following were met by a solid stone wall, which would not move aside no matter how often or in what sequence the Steward's hand movements were duplicated.

"It does not matter," a troubled Greylock said at last. "Redfrock has had the time and power to make all the changes he may have wished in this snowcastle. You will not catch him now. Therefore I declare him to be banished from this kingdom, on threat of death if he should be found or if he returns."

"What of his Familiar?" one of the soldiers, who a few minutes ago had been fighting him, asked. The crow was still flying about the room in a panic.

"Let it go. The Familiar will know what kind of master it has now."

As the doors were opened, and the bird chased from the room, Greylock turned to his allies from the BorderKeep. The Lord High Mayor looked stunned by the events, he noticed, but Harkkor was smiling broadly.

"I congratulate you, Tyrant Greylock!" the yeoman said. "You have accomplished what you set out to do."

"But not all of what I wanted to prove, Harkkor. Nor has your own problem of leadership been resolved. You realize, of course, that we were betrayed?"

The smile on Harkkor's face had disappeared, and the big man turned on the Lord High Mayor, who cringed at the sudden threat and retreated to the same wall through which the Steward had escaped, as if it would miraculously slide apart for him as well. But his retreat was stopped abruptly by the unyielding stone.

"So the left hand tunnel was the right course, Tarelton?" Harkkor said as he advanced. "You were very sure of it, and now we know why. I thought that when this time came, I would kill you gladly and without another thought. But now I foresee a better fate for you."

The yeoman reached out with a gauntleted hand and snatched the Familiar from the Lord High Mayor's shoulder. No matter how it struggled and bit, the rat could not get free, and Harkkor stuffed it into a heavy leather water bag, and sealed it tightly.

"You are no longer the Lord High Mayor, Tarelton. Your title will be simply Mayor of BorderKeep from now on, as it was before you. And you will no longer rule us—you will serve us, night and day. You will be watched, always, as we were watched, and never will you know freedom from prying eyes or our commands."

Tarelton looked relieved at this judgment, but an admiring Greylock thought that the Mayor would soon rue his reprieve, if he knew anything about the people of the BorderKeep.

There was one final matter for him to face, he thought. While the matter of his succession had been decided, he had heard the entrance of the Lady Silverfrost behind him. Now he turned to see both Silverfrost and Mara smiling at him. His heard ached at the Lady Silverfrost's beauty, and at the thought of how much he had once loved her—and desired her still. As he had feared, Mara appeared plain and skinny beside her great beauty, but he smiled as he saw the suspicious lines curl between her eyebrows as she glanced from Silverfrost to him, and back.

"Come, Mara! Sit beside me, as I promised."

An imperial and haughty Lady Silverfrost, who had always expected to be the consort of the next Tyrant—no matter who the Tyrant was—swept from the room.

As the reign of the Tyrant Greylock began, he was already suspecting that he would have more trouble from her; more than from Steward Redfrock, Mayor Tarelton, and all his other enemies put together.

Here ends the first part of the annals of Greylock of Godshome.

The second part is called Icetowers, and recounts Greylock's discovery of the secret of the Wyrrs and the finding of the true course of Gateway.